HELLO PROTOCOL FOR DEAD GIRLS

A VIRTUAL AWAKENING

ZEN DIPIETRO

PARALLEL WORLDS PRESS

COPYRIGHT

Published in the United States of America by Parallel Worlds Press

Cover art by Zen DiPietro

I DON'T REMEMBER HOW I DIED

I DON'T REMEMBER how I died. I only know that I did.

At first, I thought I was having a dream so bizarre that I had become aware of the fact that I was dreaming. One of those completely nonsensical dreams, like you're in second grade again, except your teacher is your next-door neighbor and for some reason you're wearing an aardvark for a hat, and the darn thing keeps sticking its tongue out at the wombat sitting next to you, which is really making the wombat angry.

I wish ending this could be as simple as having my alarm clock go off. But this isn't a dream.

It's not the afterlife, either.

It's a nightmare.

Last I knew, I was a college student majoring in programming. It's not conceited of me to say that I was really good at it. I had a bright future ahead of me.

There's only an abyss ahead of me now. And behind me. And everywhere else.

Since I've eliminated the possibility of this being a dream or an afterlife, that leaves only one explanation.

A wretched one. A supposedly impossible one. It's something that I was studying in school, so I can recognize the mechanics, but I never, ever expected to see it from this side. The irony of the situation hasn't escaped me, but I think that my expertise in this area is exactly why I'm able to identify what's happened.

I've never known anyone who had their memory uploaded by law enforcement after their death. It's a newer technology, which is rapidly improving, and has had a substantial effect on solving mysterious deaths and reducing the national murder rate.

People are less likely to murder someone when they know their actions could be uploaded by the police after the fact. Improvements in the technology have allowed memory upload from bodies that have been dead for twelve hours with no life support, or even partial memory recovery from a damaged brain.

The bad news for me is that memory upload only happens when a person dies under suspicious circumstances and investigators need to find out what happened.

Since I'm now trapped inside a virtual environment, my death had to be a suspicious one.

I've tried and tried to remember, but the last thing I can think of is studying for an exam in my dorm.

The death event, as it's called in the field of memory retrieval and analysis, must have been separated from everything else after the upload. Cut and pasted right out of my memory. But the rest of me is right here.

That's the big problem. I shouldn't be aware of anything. Not my death, not being inside this digital behemoth, not anything. Dead is dead.

But here I am. Formless and floating in this virtual environment. Somehow, along with my memories, they uploaded my consciousness. That isn't supposed to be possible, but here I am. Trapped. Not alive, but still existing and unable to tell anyone what has happened to me.

My name is Jennika Monroe. I'm dead, and I need to find a way out of here.

———

WHEN I FIRST REALIZED I wasn't dreaming and that I couldn't, in fact, wake up, I thought for a moment that maybe I'd reached a dark, very boring kind of heaven. Or a mild, very boring sort of hell.

But I never really bought into all that afterlife stuff, and there are things about my current situation that lead to only one possible explanation.

Data storage.

I'm very familiar with the process. I'm a—I mean I *was* a junior in college. I lived to code. I started doing it sometime around first grade. Sometimes I even thought in code. I was already working on my senior thesis project—a way of streamlining the memory analysis process so that A.I. could search for potentially traumatic events rather than relying on human review. Of course, human review would still occur, but having A.I. do the work of surveying all the mundane stuff to uncover the critical stuff would speed up the process by days or even weeks. It could mean the difference between solving a murder and having the trail go cold. It could also mean apprehending the murderer before they had time to harm someone else.

It's something I'm deeply passionate about, to the point that I didn't date or party in college. I had friends, of course, but outside my best friend Elly, they were all coders, too, and when we got together, we tended to talk about our studies.

My knowledge of all this stuff is key, I think. I hope it will give me the skills I need to let the people on the outside know I'm in here. That my body might be gone, but my mind is very much alive in here.

Entombed, in a way. This isn't supposed to be possible.

It's not even exciting. Being in here is so boring. It's like sitting inside a giant HVAC system. Even though I can't see anything, I have a sense of being surrounded by a lot of empty space, which has a lot of connections coming and going from it. I can sense when one of the connections is active. It's kind of like heat or vibration, but it's neither of those. When it happens, I sort of hear something, though it's not like anything I ever heard with my real, human ears. It's more like a buzzing sensation. There's nothing here that resembles humanity or life as I knew it. I'm certain it's data transfer, though. It's just something I feel.

That feeling of data transfer is what clued me into my status as the recently deceased.

But maybe I'm not *that* recently deceased. How would I know if years had passed? Or decades? It's not like there's a clock in here. Time is meaningless.

What about my parents? Is the loss of their only child still fresh, or have they already died of old age? My death had to be devastating for them. We were always so close. They wanted lots of kids, but ended up with just me because life sucks like that sometimes. So instead of having a house full of kids, they showered me with all the love and attention they would have given all those other kids. I can't say I'm sorry, either. It was nice. I had the best parents.

And what about Elly and Bryce? She's been my best friend since we were in kindergarten and she transferred to my school in the middle of the year. She was so quiet and sad, I shared my lunch cookies with her. My mom's chocolate chippers bought me a lifetime friendship. My cousin Bryce and I were always close, maybe because he didn't have siblings either. I'm sure Bryce and Elly are both heartbroken about my death.

It was a really nice life. Why does it have to be over? I had lots of stuff I wanted to do. Graduate. Get a job. Become a programming pioneer. Travel the world. Eat authentic food from every country in Europe and most of the ones in Asia. Fall in love and have a steamy affair. Maybe even get married.

All of that's gone and I don't even know why. I want to be angry but I'm just so confused. My thoughts twist and get recursive, almost like my own code has been corrupted.

Oh, shit. Has it? That's the only way this could get worse. Maybe that's why I can't remember how I died.

No, I can't focus on that. If my data is scrambled, then all of this is pointless anyway. I can only focus on what I *can* do.

Right.

First goal: establish a hello protocol with the outside world. Make them aware that I'm here and proceed with two-way communication.

I don't yet know what comes after that, but I can't just float around in here like some ghost. Hopefully the people out there can help me come up with the second goal.

If I just had someone to talk to, someone to understand what has happened to me, it would be so much better.

I'm so alone. I really need someone to talk to.

2

THE FIRST GOAL OF THE DEAD
GIRLS' CLUB

I'VE LEARNED how to go into sleep mode. At first, I did it on accident.

I was entertaining myself by mentally coding a shoot-em-up style game, which is the kind of thing I do to keep myself from going crazy in here. Then I suddenly realized I'd stopped doing it, and started mentally categorizing all the places I wanted to go but never had the chance to see.

I'd visited most of the big cities in the United States, but hadn't seen much of other countries. I wanted to see Paris, Beijing, and Rome in particular. But I also wanted to see the simpler places where people live quieter, everyday sort of lives.

The kind of life I'd planned to have.

Anyway, I realized that I hadn't intentionally shifted from programming the game to categorizing locations. I'd just spontaneously shifted. Some time later, that kind of shift happened again.

It sure seemed like a sort of sleep mode, so I tried to find a way to do it on purpose. After a minute or two—or a decade or two, for all I know—of trying, I succeeded.

I wish I had some concept of time. Anyway, I learned to toggle my presence on and off as desired, but it doesn't really help me.

The only other thing I can cling to in this barren existence is those data transfers I sense. It's a power fluctuation, maybe, or use of bandwidth. Whatever it is, it's like a police car, rushing along with lights and sirens blaring. It grabs my attention every time.

I dedicate myself to those power fluctuations. I make them my entire existence.

I begin to note their frequency and duration, and as I do, I learn to distinguish them. There's the high-pitched one, like ringing glass, and there's the low whirring one, like a washing machine. In between, I can discern at least a dozen other distinct types.

What does it mean? Is this some sort of data nexus? Why would it be? I should be sectioned off into cold storage —a place where data is carefully kept separate to avoid corruption. Allowing access from other areas of the system would just be dumb.

Of course, I'm not supposed to be conscious in here. So maybe that's the difference. Certainly, no one ever considered even for a moment that uploaded memories could retain a consciousness of any kind. Those memory engrams are considered entirely electrical, though embedded into physical hardware.

If anyone ever figured out how to replicate the brain in hardware form, people would be able to live forever. As it is, all we can do is upload the memories of the dead, which are like video or sound recordings.

Wait. Hang on. Something about the thing I said. Not the memory engrams or recordings or living forever, but... yes, my location. Where am I? I should be in cold storage, but what if it's some equivalent of a trash bin? What if the police, or whoever, have already gotten the data they need and I'm about to be purged?

Fear surges through me. I'm afraid, and it's not like how I experienced fear when I had a body. I don't have a pounding heart or rapid breathing. I'm not sweating. I'm...I feel like I'm elongating or stretching somehow.

What does it mean?

When a data transfer that reminds me of the rushing of water through a pipe begins, I don't even think about it. I latch onto it and use my new, stretchier sense of self to envelop it. Then I ball myself up and inject myself into it. Suddenly, I'm rushing along, like the time my parents took me sledding and we flew down hulking hills of white snow.

I only have a moment to wonder if I've made a mistake and I've hurried my way toward deletion.

"WHO ARE YOU?" a young, feminine voice asks.

Am I having a flashback or dream or something? I wish I could fling out my hands to grab onto something. I'm just so...formless. I'm like a camera view that does nothing but show a skewed perspective view with fuzzy edges.

"Are you a friend of my mommy?"

That doesn't seem like something from a dream.

I focus my attention on the question and where it came from, and am stunned to see a little girl, maybe six or seven years old, standing in the middle of a gray vignette. Her hair is in a neat brown braid down her back, and she's wearing a pink dress with short, gathered sleeves.

She seems so real.

"Can't you talk?" she asks, looking right in my direction.

Of course not. I don't have a mouth, much less a voice.

"Are you real?" I'm shocked because this was my thought, but I can hear it like words. Just like I heard her.

"No, I'm Ashta," she says with the aplomb of a child. "Do you know where my mommy is?"

"I don't," I tell her.

I'm in a tricky position because I think she's really here, just like I am. A child murder victim, maybe. It's horrible, and sad, and I don't know how to deal with that. But she somehow can speak to me, and somehow I can talk back to her, and I'm so damn glad for there to be anyone to talk to that I feel like sobbing.

"How do you have a body?" I blurt before immediately regretting my words. She can't possibly know where she is, and I don't want to tell her she's dead and never going to see her mommy.

"What do you mean? Everyone has a body." She squints at me, puzzled.

"I don't," I say.

She frowns. "If you're going to play the ghost game, you have to hide. It's the rules. It doesn't work if I can see you."

"Wait. You can see me?"

Now she gives me a look like she thinks I'm either a liar or an idiot. "Of course I can. You're right there. My eyes work just fine."

"What do I look like, then?"

She takes a step closer. "Brown hair. Blue eyes. Pretty. You have weird clothes."

"How are they weird?"

"I'm not being mean," she says defensively. "They're just all one piece, all over and kind of blue and glowy. Even your hands and feet. Nobody I know has clothes like that."

As she speaks, I become aware of something blue, and

when I direct my attention toward it, I do see a body, faintly glowing blue everywhere.

It's my body. The shape of it, anyway. I certainly never had any luminescence before.

Hands. I see hands. When I think about them, I can actually feel them.

I raise them toward me and am shocked when I feel a face. It's my face, and my hair. I can really feel them, with my hands, as if they're real.

"How did you do that?" I ask her.

"Do what?" She smiles innocently.

Does she have a body because it's the only type of existence she can understand? Does she perceive me as a person because she doesn't know any better?

But if that's all it is, why do I look like me?

I'm confused, but elated, and I don't know what to do.

"What's your name?" she asks. "I already told you mine."

"Oh. That's right, you did. I'm Jennika. And I'm so glad to meet you."

"Why?" Ashta stares at me with curious eyes.

"What?"

"Why?" the girl repeats. "Why are you glad to meet me?"

I choose my words slowly and carefully. "Well, I've been lonely and needing a friend. It's been a while since I had a friend. How about you?"

"I have lots of friends," Ashta answers. "Bennie, Crystal, Carson, Issy, NaNa, Hans, and my cousin Mika. More, too. Why don't you have friends? Do you forget to share? People don't like that."

"I always try to share," I say. "How long has it been since you saw your friends?"

"Yesterday for my birthday party. It was fun. I got this

dress." She grabs fistfuls of pink fabric to hold the dress out from her body.

"It's really pretty," I say admiringly.

Ashta doesn't seem to have any perception of time, since it isn't likely that she died just yesterday. The girl's perception of her new reality is grossly at odds with my own perception. Maybe that's just a matter of age. She's still young enough to believe in magical thinking. She can ignore things that don't make sense because to a little kid like her, most things don't make much sense.

On the other hand, her perception has bled into mine when it comes to the way I'm able to see her as a person.

Impulsively, I step forward and reach my hand out toward the child. When my hand touches her arm, it feels soft and warm, like a real child's skin.

It's just like I remember life to be.

Ashta turns her arm and puts her small hand neatly in mine. "Are we going somewhere?"

"If we were, where would we go?" I ask in a playful tone. I suddenly, desperately want to know everything Ashta knows about this place, but I have to be careful how I ask. I don't want to upset her or tip her off to the fact that she's dead.

"How about the blue room?" Ashta asks. "It looks a lot like your clothes, so you might like it."

"I don't know where that is," I tell her. "Can you show me?"

Ashta smiles, and an adorable dimple appears in her left cheek. "Sure. This way!"

She tugs me to the left.

What will I do if Ashta realizes what's really happened to her? I don't want to be responsible for a hysterical dead child. It's not like I can call her mom to calm her down and while I have decent experience with kids due to babysitting, this is way out of my league.

In spite of the risk, though, it feels indescribably humanizing to hold the girl's soft, warm little hand.

3

THE BLUE ROOM

WE START off walking toward this blue room that Ashta referred to. I feel like I'm actually swinging my legs and rolling from heel to toe with each step. After a few steps, I have a sensation of shrinking smaller, and the motion turns into more of a fluid sensation, like I'm a fast-moving cloud.

It's weird, like some sort of wonderland acid trip.

I haven't let go of Ashta's hand, but when I look down, I can no longer see it. I still feel it, though, and I maintain that grip as if my life depends on it.

Ha ha. Life. I might have to invent some new language to refer to things, since some of the phrases uttered by the living sure don't make sense for me now. It's kind of funny, and yet, on the other hand, is so very much not funny.

We drift into someplace and I feel like I'm getting bigger and growing more solid. Our hands—Ashta's and mine—reappear, still clasped together.

"See?" she asks. "The blue room." She looks very pleased with herself, having proven that she knew something I didn't.

"How did you find it?" I ask without looking at her. Instead, I'm looking at the beams of blue light running parallel and perpendicular to one another. Some of them have a pair of ninety-degree angles to direct them lower, below other sets of beams. It's like an awe-inspiring highway of light.

I try to fit what I'm seeing into what I know about how massive mainframes function. There's an answer somewhere in all this. I just need more data in order to find it.

She shrugs and balances on one foot, holding her hands out to her sides. "I just did. I got bored. I thought if I looked around a little bit, I might find my mom."

I want to ask her more pointed questions, but am afraid of upsetting her. To keep her engaged with me, I copy her stance, balancing on my right foot with my hands out to my sides. "What were you doing before you came here?"

I keep my tone light and look down at my foot because I don't want her to see any hint of how important this question is to me.

"I was at the playground," she says.

I look up at her and search her expression. She was at a playground, then she died, and her mind was uploaded here. She doesn't show any signs of distress. I don't think she knows any more about how she died than I do.

Is it routine to cut away the death event from the rest of the memory? Maybe that's the only part they keep. If so, what does that mean for the rest of me? Maybe I'm in some recycle bin right now, sitting on some cop's desktop display.

Maybe I'll blink out of existence at any moment.

I don't want that.

It might be better for me, really, than being trapped inside a machine, doomed to exist in a noncorporeal fashion like this. But I don't want to just disappear.

I want...

What do I want?

Well, I want my life back. I want to do all the things I meant to do with my life. But since that isn't an option, I at least want to figure out what happened to me and tell my parents, Bryce and Elly.

Maybe once I've been able to do that, I'll have that closure thing people talk about, and will be okay with getting purged.

It's been a while since Ashta or I said anything, but she's bouncing on her toes and doesn't seem to have noticed a lag in conversation.

I need to establish a hello protocol with the outside world.

"Ashta," I say gently. "I'm actually looking for my mom, too. I think we both got a little lost in here somehow. But I'm hoping we can help each other, and find a way to contact our moms."

"Like a phone?" she asks, a hopeful expression on her face.

"Exactly. You haven't seen anything like that, have you?"

"If I had, I would have used it," she answered tartly. "I know my phone number."

I smile at her indignance. "Of course. Silly me. You do seem to know this place a lot better than I do, though. Are there other rooms or things you can tell me about where we are?"

Ashta's face scrunches up in concentration. "Well, how much have you seen?"

"Just the last place and this one." I try to hold my hope down, but it's like wrestling a giant helium balloon to the ground.

"You haven't seen the blinky place?" Ashta asks,

surprised. "It was the first thing I saw here. I walked through the play gym tunnel and ended up in the blinky place. I tried to turn around and go back through the gym, but the door was closed or something. I couldn't get back."

"No, I didn't see a blinky place," I say. "Can you take me there?"

Ashta frowns. "I didn't like it. It's really loud. And the blinky lights were fun at first, but then they started getting on my nerves."

"But can you show me? You don't have to stay there if you don't want to." I carefully add, "It might help me figure out how to call our moms."

Ashta lets out a long breath, then nods. "Okay. I'll show you."

She reaches her hand out to me, but before my fingers can grasp hers, she disappears.

DID ASHTA just go into sleep mode? Did she get deleted?

Am I about to get deleted?

A mix of emotions rises in me. Fear, anger, and desperation leave me paralyzed with uncertainty.

I still don't know anything about where I am. My one possible source of information has evaporated. Or heck, maybe she was never even here. If I'm nothing more than some lines of code, then maybe that code is corrupted and I only imagined Ashta.

Maybe I'm just a malfunctioning program, and any second, someone's going to empty the recycle bin and I'll be truly gone, and no one will even know the difference.

"If you're going to delete me, then just do it!" I shout into the blue room.

I wait.

Nothing.

I'm still here. I have the same problem. I can't just stay in place, waiting. Even if I am crazy, I might as well be doing something.

I'm going to operate on the presumption that I'm not corrupted, because if I am, then nothing matters anyway.

Right.

The blue room.

When Ashta was here, I did see a blue glow, but now that she's gone, there's little to differentiate this place from where I was before.

Why can she see things I can't? Why do things look different when she's with me?

She's a child, and if she understands any coding at all, it would be rudimentary. So then why can she see stuff and I can't? It should be me who can see stuff.

Frankly, I'm a little pissed off about this.

Maybe she can see things because she doesn't know she shouldn't? She uses her imagination to see it. Then what? Maybe she transfers her delusion to me?

Wait. Hang on.

There's something in that. Some thread of logic that fits with something else. What is it?

Reality. Virtual reality. Perspective.

Perspective is reality.

Code is code. How that code is displayed is dependent on the hardware projecting it.

I'm the software, in this scenario. So maybe if I take this ridiculous line of reasoning one step further, that means that I can take whatever code I am, whatever I'm experiencing, and choose to display it in another fashion.

"I want to see the blue in this room." I say it out loud

rather than think it just because I can now, and there's a whole lot more that I want to start being able to do. I want to make this place, wherever I am, into my personal sandbox. I want to rule it and bend it to my will and make it mine.

Bright, glowing blue flares around me. Far more than what I saw with Ashta. This is like being bathed in a sea of light.

I can't believe that worked.

Thrilled with my success, I try again. "I want to see all the access nodes in this system."

The brightness of the blue light enveloping me dims.

Darn. I got too greedy. I should have gone with something simpler.

An image sears itself on a surface that hadn't been there before. At first, it looks like a constellation because it's all lit up in white, but there are small bits of other color too, and I recognize the image for what it is.

I'm looking at a network schematic of the entire local area network. I can see the servers, routers, switches, and, most importantly, the access nodes leading in and out.

I can see all of it.

Quivering with excitement, I map out the little bit I've seen against the bigger picture. First, where I am right now. It may be a recycle bin, but whatever this is, it's located within a server. The first place I was in, before I met Ashta, was also a server, but a bigger one. This one is for local use only, with no WAN connections that can get me outside of the local network.

Of course, I don't need to get out of the local network. I just need to get somewhere that I can get a message to some server admin who will be able to figure out what's going on.

It would help if I had more awareness of the software

running in here. Then I could see usage statistics and find something that someone will be monitoring.

Maybe I can find something like that, but at least with this schematic of the hardware, I can start creating a strategy.

One way or another, I'm going to make them hear me.

4

THE SEARCH FOR SOCKET

I'm a programmer, not a network engineer. However, in the case of hacking, the better your networking is, the better you are at hacking.

Not that I'm a hacker. Or ever wanted to be one. But my focus was always system security, and in order to protect something, I have to know how to breach it. To know my enemy, so to speak. To be able to make something strong, you have to know all the ways it could be broken.

I guess my interest in security is really helping me out now, since I know a lot more about networking than a programmer who, for example, plans to code financial software all her life.

Given my current predicament, I hesitate to call this luck, but at least it works in my favor. Given my situation, I'll take whatever I can get.

Like all networks, there are multiple ways to navigate the paths. My challenge is to find the path that will be easiest to follow while planning for something to go wrong.

That's the issue with networks. Even in the best-case scenario, a network is a patchwork of old, legacy systems which have been migrated to one thing or another, handed off to multiple teams, outsourced, insourced, retrofitted, cut back, and expanded. Multiple times over. More often than not, it's a miracle it even works, and sometimes it really shouldn't.

In other words, when you go prowling around a network, you're bound to find some crap that's been set up in the most nonsensical way possible. Sometimes a configuration is so screwed up that there's no telling why it even works. That's a big danger because a tiny change in that situation that shouldn't cause any harm can break a whole lot of stuff.

If I start trying to brute-force my way around here, I might just cause a catastrophic failure. And since my existence is predicated on these systems, I'd really prefer to avoid a failure.

I need to be cautious. That means I can't take the most direct route to my first destination: a huge server with so many connections, it has to contain some usage statistics. That data should tell me which socket I want to tap into to establish contact with the outside.

Rather than taking the quickest path to that server, I'll be going a more circuitous route, for my own protection. A lot of connections here only go one way. It's a security thing. But if I go through a one-way connection, I could end up trapped someplace I can't get out of, and then I might as well be in some kind of existential purgatory.

No, thank you. I'll make sure that wherever I go to, I can also come back from.

I take another look at the diagram in case something comes up and I need to deviate from my plan. But I know where I'm going, and I know how to get there.

At least, I know the paths to take. As for moving myself

elsewhere...I need to do it like Ashta does. She just moves place to place because she doesn't know she can't.

I hope she's in sleep mode and not deleted. I can't think about the possibility of her having been obliterated by the click of a button.

If I did, I'd have to think about the same thing happening to me.

I orient myself so I'm facing the direction I need to go, and start walking.

I'M NOT GETTING ANYWHERE. It's like one of those old-school cartoons where the characters are making a walking motion, but the background keeps recycling. My emotions cycle from worry and fear to desperation, then to frustration and anger. Finally, I settle into grim determination.

Ashta moved from place to place, and so did I when I was with her. I'm going to keep walking no matter how long it takes me to get to the next place.

I wonder where she went. I hope she's okay.

An odd tingling sensation manifests in my chest. It's kind of like when a foot falls asleep, but this is right in the center of me, and it's more intense. I feel energy building up there, or moving through me. Or doing something. It's hard to describe when I don't even know what I'm feeling. After all, I don't really have a chest. I'm guessing that the impression that I do have one is a sensory ghost attached to my memory engrams. My consciousness is interpreting the available data in ways I can understand.

That's my theory, anyway. Given that this is my first time being dead in a cyber environment, I'm relying heavily on speculation.

Hah. My best friend Elly always found my humor funny. I like to think that my mom's chocolate chip cookies wooed her into being my friend, but my tendency to be verbose, along with my irreverence for pretty much everything, made her stick around.

I couldn't have asked for a better friend. She was like a sister I got to choose. I was as comfortable in her parents' house as I was in my own, and vice versa. We even went to the same college, and jumped through a lot of hoops to be able to share a room. The college administrators didn't want to let us do it, but Elly's uncle was an influential alumnus, and he made a few calls on our behalf. Plus, she and I called every day. I think, more than anything, we wore them down until they gave in just so we would go away and leave them alone.

We had so much fun together, and we didn't even have to do much to have a blast. We watched movies, had impromptu dance parties, helped each other through dating nightmares and unrequited crushes, and most of all, we laughed.

I want to let her know I'm not gone. Not entirely. She must be sick with grief. I know I would be if I was the one left behind. What must it be like for her to live in our dorm room with my absence screaming at her? She'll probably ask for a different room. She should.

Hang on. My thoughts wandered off and the tingly feeling stopped. I get my bearings and pay attention to where I am.

Did I go into sleep mode? I feel like I blinked out and came back. Maybe that's how it happens—thinking too much about my real life.

Maybe it makes me recede into my own code?

It feels true. I don't know if that means anything.

I wish I had some sort of user manual for being a disembodied consciousness trapped inside a memory storage device. I mean, I've never read a user manual for anything before, but that would be one worth the effort, I think.

Okay, tingly feeling. Come back. Let's move this along. I have things to do.

I start walking again, envisioning my arrival in another place.

It's back! I feel the tingle and the flowing, sliding sort of feeling I had when moving from one place to another with Ashta.

Something different forms around me. At first, I'm not sure what to make of it, but it's different, and right now different is good.

This place is weird, though.

It's like I'm on a highway, but instead of being a highway, it's a tunnel, and it's dark, and instead of vehicles passing me, they're bright lights. Each light zings by at a crazy fast rate, making it look to me like a very linear shooting star streaking right by me.

And the sound.

The lights make sound as they go by, and I've never heard anything like it. It's a vibrating sort of hum but enclosed, as if it's going through a tube and getting muffled. The sound intensifies as the lights approach, then recedes as they go by.

It's trippy. But kind of cool, in a way.

One of them flies right at me, coming from nowhere, and I don't have time to get out of the way. Instead, instinctively, I reach for it. Stupid. For all I know, this junk will corrupt me.

But it's already in my hand and it isn't glowing anymore. I carefully release my fist and peer between my fingers.

It's a data packet. A small chunk of code. When it arrives at its destination, it will join up with its pals to form whatever it's meant to be. An email or a file or whatever.

I look at where the packets are coming from, then track their paths across the space. Wherever they're going is where I want to go. They'll be headed deeper, to the TCP network layer.

Does that align with what I had planned based on the network layout?

Seems like it.

I hold my hand up, palm open, and nudge the inert packet with my finger.

It leaps out of my hand and flies in the same direction as the rest of them, as if being drawn by a super magnet. It makes a muffled *whoompf* sound as it goes, like when you put a cylinder into one of those parcel-delivery vacuum tubes.

"All right, packet," I say. For some reason, it's comforting to speak. It reminds me that I'm human in this very inhuman place. "I'll follow you."

I start off in that direction, wondering what the next place will be like. I haven't the faintest inkling of what I might experience. I kind of hope that I end up in a spot that's all white with shiny surfaces and reverberating with a sound that's like angels are singing in chorus. Just because it would be kind of cool. Like in a movie.

Oddly, instead of just morphing into a new environment, I see that the packets are zooming into a round opening at shoulder height.

I look at my entirely digital body, then at the opening. Even if the two things were physical, I'd be able to fit.

All right. Let's give it a whack.

I reach up, planning to do a leap that will get my upper

body onto the ledge, then scramble to get the rest of myself in.

A dark shape appears, shoving me away.

I stumble back, surprised. Am I getting smacked down by some sort of virus protection?

If that's the case, this system's virus protection looks like a young woman around my age, wearing her hair in a long ponytail down her back.

She looks distinctly unhappy. "You can't go there."

"Why?" I ask.

"Because you'll die."

5

BUT WE'RE ALREADY DEAD

AGAIN, I find myself in the position of having to decide whether I should inform someone that they've died or keep that information to myself.

While Ashta had been sweet and friendly, this girl seems angry. The snap in her eyes and tightness of her mouth suggest she'd just as soon have me dead, and I have to wonder why she bothered to warn me against something that could kill me.

Since I'm already dead, my existence is beginning to mean something else to me. I'm not sure what yet. It isn't life. What does it mean to exist without being alive?

"Are you stupid?" The girl spits the words at me.

"I guess that's a matter of opinion," I say carefully. "What's in there?"

I indicate the opening with a glance.

"Why should I tell you?" she demands.

"I don't know. You bothered to tell me not to go in. That must count for something. And we aren't exactly surrounded by a lot of people here. Our options for socializing are limited."

She frowns. "Have you seen any others?"

"A young girl. Now you. That's it."

"Are you new?" she asks.

"I don't know," I answer honestly. "I'm trying to figure things out."

I take a chance on introducing myself to her. "I'm Jennika."

"Good for you." She glares at me.

Was she this unpleasant when she was alive? I hope not. As far as electronic ghosts go, she's kind of a jerk.

Elly would know how to handle this girl. There isn't a person on Earth Elly can't charm with her big smile and gentle personality.

Elly always puts her focus on the other person. I'll try that.

"Have you had a hard time here?" I ask. "Is there anything I can help you with?"

Her eyes narrow suspiciously. "Why?"

"Why what?"

"Why would you want to help me? Is this a trick?"

"No," I say slowly. "I mean, if I were trying to pull something, I'm sure I'd lie and say no anyway, so I'm sure you can't believe me when I say no. But I don't have anything to gain by tricking you."

She looks at me, her gaze full of naked distrust.

I think kindness is the wrong way to go with her.

"Don't get me wrong," I continue. "If chucking you into that hole would help me out in some way, I'd do that, and I imagine you'd do the same to me. But you didn't, so I'm guessing there's nothing to be gained by it."

She's still eyeing me like I'm a Labrador with its eyes on her burger, but her energy has calmed.

Huh. Now that I think about it, it is her energy I'm

reacting to more than her expressions and body language. Before, she was generating a choppy, overclocked feeling, but that has eased.

Am I learning to perceive things in here the way they really are, rather than subconsciously translating it into something more human?

I don't know if that's a good thing or a scary thing.

"We don't have to work together," I tell her when she doesn't respond. "I can just keep moving through. I just thought that if we shared what we know, it might help us figure things out."

"You think so?" she asks.

"I think it can't hurt. And I also think this place has some bizarre characteristics. Don't you? The little girl didn't know anything was wrong, but you have to know that all this isn't right."

"Are you real?" she asks me.

"I don't know how to answer that," I say. "What's real? I'm a university student, I can tell you that. With a real name. Jennika. Like I told you. I have a best friend named Elly, and my cousin Bryce is just like another best friend. I love tacos and hate green peppers. What else do you want to know?"

For the first time, she looks uncertain of herself. "I don't know. Like you said, if you're just a figment of my imagination, you'll just say whatever I might believe."

"You think you're imagining me?" I ask.

"It's the only thing that makes sense. I'm dreaming or in a coma or something. Stuck inside my mind."

I'm intrigued, wondering how she came to this conclusion. She has a grasp on reality that Ashta doesn't have, but she doesn't know what I know about memory upload.

"What about an afterlife? I considered that possibility for about half a second."

For the first time, her frown eases. She looks faintly amused, though she doesn't smile. "I don't believe in that stuff. And if an afterlife existed, it would either be a whole lot better or a whole lot worse than this. It wouldn't be so... so much nothing."

"I like your reasoning," I say.

Her expression tightens up again.

I meant what I said, but she probably thinks I'm just trying to flatter her. "I don't know how to convince you that I'm real, and that I'm not a jerk. I guess I'd have to do something you wouldn't imagine I'd do, but since I don't know you, I have no idea what that would be. It puts me in a tight spot, you know?"

She doesn't respond. She just keeps watching me with the expression of someone watching a bug walk across the floor. Like she doesn't know if she wants to squash me or not.

I sigh. "Well, it's not like we have to be friends. Good luck to you."

I turn back to the opening that originally caught my interest. The one that should lead me closer to the place where I can find out where I need to go to contact the outside.

"Don't," she says, her voice loud and full of tension.

I turn back to her. "Why? This is where I need to go."

"Someone else went that way, and then I heard screaming, and she never came back." She speaks with great reluctance, looking down at her feet. It's the first sign of vulnerability I've seen from her.

"Screaming?" I repeat, looking at the opening.

"Yeah."

"Maybe it was good screaming?" I suggest hopefully. "Like, yay, I came through this hole and everything in here is just so super great."

Her gaze snaps up to me. "It most definitely was not a happy sound."

"Hmm." I don't love the possibilities, but given what I know, there's no reason for me to find something over there that will make me scream. "It wasn't a little girl, was it?"

Whatever this girl witnessed, I hope it didn't happen to Ashta.

"No. You met a little girl here?"

"Yeah. I'm not sure if she's still here, though."

She asks, "Where would she go?"

"I don't know," I say. It's true. I don't *know*. I only *suspect* the possibility of deletion. "What did you know about the girl who went through?"

She blinks as if the question required her to change the direction of her thoughts. "Not much. Short, curly hair. Some kind of accent. She was a little weird."

"Weird how?" I press.

"I don't know. Kind of twitchy. Nervous, I guess."

"Well, that could make sense. This isn't a normal situation," I point out.

"That's all I know. She came through here, went in there, and that was the last I saw of her."

"Have you seen anyone else?"

She shakes her head. "No. Just her, then you."

I wish I knew how long she's been here in comparison to how long I've been here. There are at least four of us in here. Or there were.

"How old was she?" I ask.

"I don't know, sixteen or seventeen, maybe. Younger than us."

"How old are you?"

She frowns, and seems like she won't answer, but then she says, "Twenty."

"Same here," I say, distracted, reviewing what little I know. Four girls, ranging from Ashta's age to twenty. It's not a large enough sample size to draw any significant conclusions.

"You're going through there no matter what I say, aren't you?" she asks.

"Yes."

She runs her hands down the front of her shirt. "Fine. Then I'll go first."

"Hang on. What?"

She steps closer, fixing me with that steely self-assurance that seems to be her trademark. "I don't want to be left standing here alone while I don't know what happens. So if something terrible happens, it will happen to me and you'll have to listen to it."

I return her gaze. "That's a very unexpected conclusion."

"I'm a very unexpected kind of person." She pushes past me and reaches up to the opening. "Are you going to follow me?"

"Yep."

"Even if I start screaming?"

"Yep."

"Okay then." She bends her knees, then jumps, pulling herself with her arms as she does, landing her stomach on the ledge of the opening.

I hear her voice. "Make yourself useful. Grab my feet and push, will you?"

"Sure." I move around to grasp her ankles and push her forward. She must be using her arms because she slides away, into the opening, then falls out of view.

I'M LISTENING. Cringing.

I don't hear any screaming. That's good.

I hope that's good.

I just stand there, listening, for a span of time that starts to stretch out too long.

All right. My turn. I reach up and simultaneously jump and pull myself up into the ledge. The next bit is awkward, since there's no one to push me through. I wish I could have gotten up here and climbed in feet-first, but this virtual environment is entirely without ladders or stepstools.

The idea amuses me, even as I awkwardly rock my hips side to side and drag myself on my belly with my hands.

Abruptly, the ledge falls away and I drop straight down. I curl up, waiting for a horrible, hard landing.

It doesn't come. I open my eyes and realize I'm not moving. I'm already lying on something. Also, the light has gotten a lot brighter. It's a bright, artificial white. Cautiously, I unfurl myself and raise up on my left elbow.

"What took you so long?" The girl whose name I still don't know steps around me, looking curious and only somewhat annoyed. "I've been waiting for you forever."

I wish either of us had some objective measure of time. As far as I can tell, it's only been a minute since she came through the opening. But maybe I went into sleep mode and I didn't know it. Or maybe she did. Or maybe we just perceive time differently.

"Got here as fast as I could." I stand up. "What have you found?"

"I wish I knew." She turns her head to her right and upward, and I follow her gaze.

If where we are qualifies as a room, then the ceiling is covered with a rushing highway of...I don't know what.

It's light and energy streaking by like a digital fireworks show.

"What is it?" she asks softly.

"Reality," I say.

"What is reality?" She looks at me. "What does it mean that we're here?"

My heart breaks to tell her the truth, but something about her tells me that pretty lies are the wrong way to go. Whatever life she's led, it's been about hard truths and realities, and she needs to know what's really happening.

"Something happened to us," I say. "We died. These aren't our real bodies. Our memories have been uploaded into a police mainframe, and somehow, our consciousnesses came with it. The police don't know we're here."

Her forehead creases, and I know that she doesn't doubt what I'm saying.

"Do you remember anything?" she asks. "About how you died."

"No," I say. "Do you?"

"No." She meets my gaze, and for the first time, I feel like we could be something like friends. Maybe not friends exactly, but maybe we could work together to figure things out.

"How do you know?" Her voice sounds toneless and hollow. Resigned. Almost like she expected something like this, but finding out for sure has nonetheless broken her spirit.

"I'm a programmer," I say. "At least, I was studying to be one. I didn't have a job at it or anything. But I found a layout for this system's specifications, and I'm looking for a way to let them know we're here. That we're aware, I mean. We're not supposed to be, but we are."

"Memory upload?" she asks faintly. "Like...the thing they've been talking about on tv. Which means someone killed us?"

"Probably," I say gently. "We're not really here. Not the way we feel like we are, with bodies and everything. We're just perceiving it that way to normalize the data we're receiving."

"How?" she asks, still sounding vacant. "How does that make sense?"

"I don't know," I admit. "I wish I had all the answers, but I'm still looking, like you are. Trying to find an answer."

"If we're dead," she says slowly, her gaze meeting mine, "then what do answers matter?"

"Don't you want to know what happened to you?" I asked. "To tell someone that you're still here, or at least tell them goodbye?"

Her gaze drifts off somewhere behind my left shoulder. Slowly, her head moves from side to side. "No. I can guess what happened, more or less. I don't need the details. And there's no one who would care."

She looks so lost, like becoming aware of her death has instantly morphed her into a ghost of her former, forceful self.

"I'm Jennika," I say, because I want to call her by her name to let her know that I see her and acknowledge her existence. But I don't know her name. "Who are you?"

"No one," she whispers. "I'm no one. I never was."

There's something so naked and haunted and lost about her that tells me that she led a life completely opposite of mine. I was loved and protected. I sense she never had anyone. Yet here we are, both together in this same place.

Taking a risk, I reach out my hand to her. "We're both no one now, together. Maybe you didn't have anyone who would be there for you in life, but it's just you and me in here right now, and I'll be here for you, for whatever our existence brings."

She doesn't move, and I take that as encouragement that the promise of my touch hasn't repulsed her. I've never felt so uncertain of myself, but I reach out and grasp her hand.

"I'm Jennika," I say again. "Your new sister, and I promise, I won't leave you as long as I have any say about it."

Her eyes are wide and I don't know if they're full of fear or hope or what, but her grip on my hand tightens slightly.

Her other arm comes forward and I flinch from the blow she's about to deliver. But then it doesn't happen that way. Instead, her hand finds my shoulder, then her arm wraps around me and I find myself inside the hug of a girl I don't know but who has become the only person in my life.

No, not my life. I'm already dead. She's the only person in my existence.

We cling to each other, and my neck is wet with her tears. Whether they're tears of grief for her lost life or tears of relief for having someone, I don't know, but I feel like I'm crying, too, because I no longer feel so alone and right now, that's everything to me.

"Daiya," she whispers.

"What?"

"My name's Daiya."

ALMOST IMMEDIATELY, Daiya straightens, smears her hands over her cheeks, and puts on her game face.

At least, I assume that's her game face. It's equal parts

grim determination and suicidal hostility with just a sprinkling of nervousness.

It's impressive and a little unnerving.

"So now what?" Her voice is strong again and shows none of the brief vulnerability she'd shown.

"If what I saw was accurate, then this is a router."

"A what?" Her expression is blank.

She's clearly not familiar with networking. There's no real reason she should be, but it will make explaining things harder. "The details don't matter much," I say. "This is just a place where signals from different directions get sent this way or that way. It's like, um, a bus station. Traffic gets routed this way or that way. This place doesn't have anything we want. We're going that way." I point ahead. "The server I want should be that way."

Daiya nods slowly. "Okay. So how do we get there?"

"To be honest, I was kind of hoping there would be some opening or blinking light or something kind of obvious. I'm not seeing anything. Are you?"

She turns around slowly, her head tilted back, scanning everything. "Not a damn thing."

She sighs. "Are we really inside a computer?"

"Yeah," I say. "We really are."

She stretches her hands out in front of her, looking at them. "And our bodies aren't real?"

"No. They're some kind of residual self-image."

"Think I can make myself taller?" she asks.

Of all the things she might have said about adapting to a digital existence, this was not one of the things I anticipated. "Why?"

"I always wanted to be taller. And if this isn't real anyway, shouldn't I be able to change it?"

It sounded reasonable to me. "I guess you could try."

Her eyes narrow in concentration and her face grows increasingly strained. Finally, she blows out a breath and shakes her head. "Guess not. Unless I look taller?"

I shake my head regretfully. "Afraid not."

"Darn." A small smirk shows that she has a quirky sense of humor, which, in this case is a good thing.

I need her to be able to handle the bizarre and the seemingly impossible, because I don't know if I can do this without help.

Heck, I don't know if I can do it *with* help. Theoretically, Daiya and I aren't supposed to be in here along with our memories, so given that we're already doing the supposedly impossible, any further theorizing and supposition really is just a time waster.

"Before," I say, "when I was going from one place to another, I just imagined going and moved in that direction. If it worked then, it should work now, right?"

Daiya looks less than convinced, but she shrugs. "Let's give it a try."

I reach for her hand, but as my fingers graze hers, she yanks her hand away.

"I just want to make sure we stay together," I say. "Some kind of connection, maybe, will keep one of us from going astray somehow."

"You think?"

I shrug. "No idea. I'm making this up as I go. But when writing code, a simple 'and' can be a very powerful thing. Just that one little thing can break things or fix them."

I hold out my hand.

Looking extremely dubious, she takes it.

Together, we walk forward.

We bump into the wall.

"Okay, so that didn't work." I bite my lip, trying to think what to try next.

"Can we stop holding hands now?" Daiya asks dryly.

"No," I say, and to be honest, I'm mostly lying. I just want to pay her back a little bit for her snarky attitude.

The answer to why we couldn't get through hits me. "We hit a firewall. Crap. It seems we can't just go wherever we want. We won't be able to get into areas we don't have permissions for."

Daiya frowns. "So how do we get permissions?"

"Some network admin person would have to give them to us. And if we could get in touch with someone like that, then that would be all we need. So that's not helpful."

"Okay," Daiya says slowly, thinking. "So how does whatever-it-is know that we don't have permissions?"

"Access usually happens via login, but there's no way I can just hack that."

"But we're nothing," she says. "Just electrical currents, or code, or whatever. Can't we just make ourselves into what it wants?"

"No, we—" I stop abruptly. By oversimplifying something very complicated, she may have just come up with a great idea.

I look up at the routers above us.

Daiya follows my gaze. "Whatever I said that's making you think whatever you're thinking, I take it back."

"No, it's a great idea," I say, injecting enthusiasm into my voice to hopefully come across as highly convincing.

She doesn't need to know that I have no idea what I'm doing.

"What, exactly, is a good idea?" She's low-key tugging her hand away, but I hold fast.

I point upward. "All we need to do is identify a packet

that's going where we want to go, and jam ourselves into it. It already has the right permissions, by nature of what it is."

"How do we know where it's going?"

"I'll have to identify the right path. Then whatever's going that way will be whatever we hitch a ride on."

"And if we can't get off, or out, or whatever?" she demands.

"I don't know," I admit. "I've never been dead and trapped inside a cyber environment. I'm kind of working it out as I go."

She glares at me as if I'm the source of all her troubles. I don't take it personally. I'd love to have someone to blame for everything, too.

Blame can be a very useful mechanism. Elly, Bryce and I used to have a system for it. If the three of us had been hanging out, and one of us left, then that person became the sole cause of everything we did that our parents didn't like.

Who didn't close the garage door? Who scuffed the floor? It was convenient to blame anything messy or destructive on Bryce, since he's the most likely to do that anyway. He's tall with a big build and tends not to know his own strength. Of course, we had to clean up, fix, or replace whatever we'd blamed on the missing third person, but having someone who was not present to blame it on avoided a lecture from whichever parental figure was on duty at the time.

We all took our turns being the blamed.

I look at Daiya, and she has a weird expression. "What?"

"Where did you go?" she asks.

I realize she's let go of my hand. "What do you mean? I was just remembering something."

"No, you left. You were gone for a while."

I stare at her. "Left? As in, you couldn't see me anymore?"

"No, left as in you went really far to the left and just kept going left until you were the leftiest lefter who ever lefted. Yes, I'm saying I couldn't see you anymore!"

Daiya's funny when she's mad.

"How long was I gone?" I ask.

"I don't exactly have a watch."

"Well, did it feel like a long time?"

She scowls. "You didn't blink out and come right back. I had plenty of time to wonder about this place you've gotten me stuck in, and think about what I'd do next."

"Did you decide anything?"

"I was thinking I'd go back through the hole. Maybe see where else I might be able to poke around."

"Going back wouldn't help us," I say. "We'd just be moving from useless place to useless place."

"Maybe for you," she says. "We don't have the same goal, I don't think. It's not like I have anyone I'm trying to say my goodbyes to. My boss at the convenience store would have just assumed I'd quit, and find someone to replace me. My old social worker would eventually track down what happened to me, maybe feel a little sad, then go right on about her life. Kids who age out of foster care end up in the morgue at a much higher rate than the average."

I've never seen someone look so bitter.

"At least we can let someone know we're in here," I tell her. "At least that would be something, right?"

But she's gone. Like a light turning off, she's simply not where she was a moment ago.

She was thinking of her past. That's what happened to me, too. When we think about the lives we had, we go into some dormant state or sleep mode or something.

Well, crap. How long is she going to be gone? I don't want to leave her behind, but I feel like I can't just wait around, either. For all I know, years are slipping away, and my parents, Elly, and Bryce might die of old age before I get the chance to make contact with the outside world.

I'll briefly wait for Daiya, but then I'll have to move on and try to find her again later.

I focus my attention on the routers above me, and the paths going into and out of them. Without the network design in front of me, I can't tell for sure what's what.

One by one, I look at the largest paths going from the routers in the direction I want to go. They have different feels to them. Everything here has a sort of frequency—a humming, vibrating energy. Some are slow and steady, some are fast and intermittent. Most are somewhere between.

How am I supposed to pick one without sufficient information? I've never been one for just flinging myself into something willy-nilly. I like a logical sequence of events. This seems like a particularly bad time for me to start being reckless.

On the other hand...what do I have to lose? I'm already dead. Living responsibly sure didn't increase my time on Earth. Maybe doing something impulsive and reckless just this once might work in my favor. I can try it out and avoid exposing Daiya to any potential hazards. She seems like she's been through enough already. She doesn't need me adding to her difficulties.

Right. I'll pick one of these paths, climb in, and see what happens. If it works out, I'll come back for Daiya. Hopefully, she'll be back soon. If not, then I'll have to think about really moving on without her for now.

Which path? I don't have any objective means of choosing. Nothing about any of the pathways leading in the direction of the server calls to me. Which one appeals to me, then?

There's one that has a somewhat constant, higher-pitched hum, and it reminds me of my parents' refrigerator.

Is that a good enough reason to select one path over another? In the absence of any other indicator, I decide to just go with my choice before I have a chance to talk myself out of it.

I reach up to it, imagining myself walking toward it and colliding with it.

A strange sensation consumes me. It reminds me of the pull of water when draining a bathtub, but my whole body is feeling it.

I'm inside a rushing, sliding cloud. No, that's not exactly right. It seems like I'm *surrounded* by a cloud while going down a water slide. When I was alive, I loved roller coasters and water parks, so I bet I'd have loved this, if I wasn't so terrified about what's happening to me.

Why didn't I wait for Daiya? If she or Ashta had been with me, I would have felt responsible for their wellbeing, and I wouldn't have done this.

I wasn't so impulsive when I was alive. Death has changed me, I guess.

With an odd zapping sensation, I suddenly fall out of the tube and find myself...somewhere.

Unfortunately, I can't be more specific because experiencing a computer network from the inside has absolutely nothing to do with what it looks like on the outside.

I have few clues to work with.

A horrible sound assaults me and I shrink down, covering my ears, only to realize that this isn't an external sensation. It's happening in my head, or whatever it is I have that passes for a head these days.

6

BOSS OF THE UNKNOWN

You stupid idiot, where did you go?

Bright lights flash and suddenly, Daiya's standing in front of me, looking at me like she'd kill me if I weren't already dead.

She opens her mouth to continue berating me, but I hold up my hand.

I say, "You can yell at me some more in a minute, but first, how did you do that? Did you come through the tube?"

"Do what? And what tube?"

"How did you make me hear you when you were somewhere else, and how did you get here?"

She scowls at me, and for a minute, I think she's going to hit me. Interestingly, I don't flinch away because I know that whatever she does, she won't actually be hitting me. It will only seem that way, but it won't be real.

I think I'm starting to adjust to an altered plane of existence, just a little.

But she doesn't strike out at me. "One second, you were standing there and the next second, you were gone, so I just focused on you and got mad. I blipped in here."

She shrugs.

"Blipped?" I repeat.

"What else do I call it?" she asks. "I was in the other place, I thought about how I wanted to wring your neck, and it felt like a rubber band snapping me to here."

"Huh." I wish I had something smarter to say, but I really don't.

"Why did you leave?" Her voice is angry, but it's not telling the truth. She felt scared and abandoned.

Of course she did. She spent her life as a foster kid, being kicked out and passed to someone else on a regular basis.

I shouldn't have left without her.

"You went into some sort of sleep mode," I said. "You disappeared, and I was the one who was alone. I thought I'd check something out while I waited for you to come back. I didn't ditch you. I swear."

"What do you mean, sleep mode?" she asks. The false anger has dissipated and now she just seems forlorn and uncertain.

I say, "Were you thinking about your life, before I appeared to be missing? Be careful. Don't start thinking what you were thinking then, or you might blink out again."

"Yeah," she says cautiously. "I was."

"I suspect that when we think about our lives, we go into some kind of data loop that puts our active consciousness into some kind of sleep mode," I tell her. "So we need to be careful about getting nostalgic."

She purses her lips thoughtfully, then peers at me curiously. "Do you think that's how it's supposed to work? They upload us here, and we just dwell on our memories while they pick them apart?"

I hadn't thought of that, but it makes sense. "Maybe."

"Well then that kind of sucks," she says. "We need to make contact with them to let them know what they're doing to people. It isn't okay to torture us this way."

Is this torture?

I like to think I've handled this turn of events well, but would it have been more humane to just let my memories and consciousness disappear?

Probably. I ache to contact my parents, Elly, and Bryce, and that's probably nothing compared to someone who was in love or had children.

I try to imagine if I had someone special in the living world, someone I'd made promises to. Knowing that they were grieving over me and wanting to get back to them to take care of them would probably rip me to shreds.

Yeah, this could be a form of torture, in some circumstances.

Maybe even for me, if I never manage to contact the outside world. What should I do then? Continue banging around in here until they decide to delete my data? Hope they'd finally put an end to me? Or would I be dreading that idea?

I don't know what's worse.

"We do need to make contact," I agree. "In order to do that, we need to figure out where we are. Or, at least, how to get to my intended destination in the server."

"Okay." Daiya looks around. "How do we do that?"

"Good question."

"You didn't have a plan?" She stares at me.

"Well, I did," I say defensively. "But it was a loose plan, as in, get here and see what it is. It's not like I have experience with what we're trying to do. As far as I know, it's never been done."

She mutters, "I never intended to be a trailblazer."

For some reason, this strikes me as funny, and I involuntarily snort out a strange, short laugh.

She gives me a sideways, startled look, then smirks. "So, what should I be doing here?"

Her tone has softened, and she sounds almost friendly.

"Find a way out. Or in. Or figure out what's passing through. Or...something." I wish I had a better answer.

"Right." She nods. "We're winging it. Well, you're in luck. Kids who've spent their lives in the system are experts at winging it."

The noise was the first thing I noticed here, because it's dark and loud. But now that I focus my attention, I can see a floor and walls. I don't know what these things represent, since I'm not actually in a room of any sort, but there are structures spanning the walls, traversing almost the entire length of a wall, and moving upward.

Daiya shrugs, puts a foot on the bottom structure, and reaches up.

"I don't know if you should do that," I say.

"What else is there to do?" she counters, not even pausing as she climbs up ledge after ledge.

She's brave. I admire that. She doesn't have my knowledge of virtual environments, but she's not letting that hold her back. She's pushing forward in the only way she knows how.

I'm starting to like her.

The sound around me goes from a cacophony and condenses down to a weird, vibrating hum.

Daiya reaches the top of the wall. "There's a thing here. I'm going to grab it."

"Wait!" I shout, but it's too late. She grabs hold of what looks like a glowing wire, then she's glowing, and her glow begins to flow into the wire's glow.

Then she's gone.

"Well, shit." I have to follow her. It's my fault she did that. But I don't know what happened to her, or what will happen to me, and what if I'm just following her into some virus quarantine, which will be one short hop away from permanent deletion?

On the other hand...so what if that's what happens? I'm dead. I'm supposed to be gone. Who's to say that wiping out my consciousness wouldn't be better for me in the long run?

I try to convince myself of that, but the truth is, my desire to continue to exist, in whatever form is possible, outshines my practicality. I don't want to disappear.

But I'm going to follow Daiya anyway.

I huff out a fake breath, which I know is fake because I don't have a real body, then I reach for the first segment on the wall and begin climbing.

Too soon, I arrive at the top, just as she had, and just as she did, I reach out and touch the glowing wire.

A shattering sensation explodes through me, as if I'm made of electric glass and every bit of me has broken down into billions of atoms.

Then I feel a wild sensation like I've been flung from a catapult.

7

E=MC2

AFTER A SLINGSHOT RIDE, I find myself smack in the middle of something that feels innately familiar.

If I were to imagine what it felt like to be inside a server, this would tick all the boxes. There's a sensation of permanence, like grandma's basement stuffed with ancient, dusty stuff that will never see the light of day again. But there's also a feeling of movement. Traffic. There's a lot of energy here.

Is it the server I've been trying to reach?

There's only one way to find out.

Daiya's standing in the center of it all. "Wow," she says, turning slowly. "It's like a planetarium on an acid trip."

There are connections lights and a feeling like subways rushing by in multiple directions all at once. I don't know that I'd think of it as a planetarium, but now that she's mentioned it, it does have a vast, cosmic sort of feel.

Before I died, I would have considered this to be an amazing experience, as epic as actually going out into space.

Now, though, all this digital confusion is starting to piss

me off. I'm ready to get to the point and make some stuff happen.

"Stay where you are and don't touch anything," I tell her.

"Why?"

"I'm going to do something stupid."

To her credit, she's unfazed. "Cool. Good luck."

I nod. "Thanks."

I locate the area that seems to be burning the hottest and approach it.

Most people don't realize how hot and loud data centers are. They think a data center is just a room that quietly hums with lots of computer equipment, and maybe some cool blinky lights.

Hardly. A big data center serves the entire world. It's huge, and it's so noisy that you can't hear the person next to you speaking unless they're screaming and even then, it's hard. These places are hot, too, despite the tremendous efforts made to cool them.

The area that has caught my special interest isn't burning hot because it's getting more traffic. It's burning hot because it's critical. It has multiple failsafes running, simultaneously.

Though there are probably hundreds of servers in the vicinity, this one, I believe, is a critical juncture for the system itself.

I'm pretty sure I'm at ground zero for this entire environment, and my objective has changed. Before, I wanted only to get a map of the infrastructure. This place is too much of an opportunity to be tentative, though.

One way or another, I'm going to make them notice me.

I take everything I am, and was, and I stretch it, expand it, double it back over itself, and make whatever I've become into a weapon.

I stab myself right into the eye at the center of all this and merge myself into it.

8

BRUTE FORCE METHOD INITIATED

I AM CODE.

Somehow, in this new iteration of myself, I don't have to write code anymore. I think it, then I become it.

In this case, I'm making myself into a query, and I'm searching all possible connections to find the statement that will match my query.

Detect me. Talk to me. That's what it all boils down to. I want to make the people on the outside recognize that something's going on in here, and that they need to interface with it. With me.

I run through pathway after pathway that doesn't support the function I'm searching for. I don't know how much time this is taking, since I haven't yet synced up with a time stamp, but Daiya has blinked in and out four times during the process.

Interestingly, I'm now looking both internally and externally. Internally at the systems, and externally at my false perception of my surroundings—including Daiya.

If I were her, I'd be going nuts waiting, but she seems to be waiting patiently, in standby mode.

Then I find a match to my query. A connection opens between me and a port that interfaces directly with the end user on a regular basis.

That port runs a backup protocol every two hours and informs the administrator, or admin, that the backup was successful. It's a process that's expected to always work and is taken for granted. But should it fail, all hell would break loose.

It takes laughably little effort for me to cause the backup to fail. Like the twitch of an eye.

I focus my attention on Daiya for the first time in I don't know how long and smile.

She looks surprised by my sudden attention. "What?"

"I've sent up a signal flare, so to speak. They'll be in touch soon."

"Really?" She wears a look of sudden awe. "How?"

"Any attempt for them to reinitialize the backups will come directly to me. They will query me directly and a dialogue will be established. We'll finally be able to say hello."

"Hello, my ass," Daiya blurts out. "I want to tell them to fix the mess they've made."

A second query comes back positive.

Daiya's perceptive and knows something has happened. "Did they say hello?"

"Not yet," I say, "but we'll know how long it takes. I've synced with a universal clock, so we can track time now."

For some reason, I feel suddenly almost human again. Funny how the mere awareness of time makes me feel centered in reality.

"The clock is ticking, admin," I say aloud. "How long will you let those backups continue to fail?"

9

HELLO, BITCHES

I FEEL like a butterfly emerging from a chrysalis, my wings still wet but unfurling. I keep writing queries and establishing connections with access points. Each new connection is like a new weapon added to my arsenal, and I am absolutely preparing to go to war, if it comes to that.

I hope it doesn't come to that.

I now know which system I'm in. I knew that it had to be run by a highly sophisticated operation, and I was right about that. Boston Mitigated Technical Solutions, Inc—more commonly known as BomiTech—is an information technology juggernaut and the company contracted to work with law enforcement agencies across the country. It makes perfect sense that they'd have the contract for memory upload. While that means I'm in a highly stable, well-maintained environment, it also means that the best of the best IT professionals will be the ones I have to fight.

On the plus side is the fact that today's date is only two weeks after the last memory I have of studying in my dorm. That means that it isn't too late to find out what happened to me. It also means that my loved ones haven't been mourning for years while unaware that I'm still here.

I want to know how long Daiya's been here, but I'm reluctant to ask her about the last thing she remembers. Since she didn't know she was dead before she met me, I doubt she has any memory of her demise. Asking her to reminisce about her life might be unpleasant for her.

At some point, though, I'll need to know. I'll have to think of a way to broach the subject in a tactful way.

Tact has never been my strong suit. It was always Elly who filtered things for me, softening them up to get my point across while looking after our classmates' feelings. She taught me a lot about how to relate to others without hurting feelings, and I often think about how she would handle something to help me figure out the best way.

We always said we'd be friends forever. Since our friendship has officially transcended death, it seems we weren't being grandiose.

The more I work with this server, the more I learn. I'm the Marco Polo of memory storage.

I've watched the flow of data, noted what's interacting with what, and run numerous queries. I have a knowledge of this server that even the engineer who designed it and the admin who looks after it can't begin to fathom.

It gives me an odd little thrill of power.

I'm not an egomaniac or anything. It's just that I've felt so lost and discarded and helpless that getting a handle on my surroundings is a heady feeling.

"Anything?" Daiya sits quietly. She doesn't understand what's going on. She has no understanding of computers beyond the button that turns them on and off. That's fine, most people don't. But it means that I must translate what's happening into a way she can grasp.

"They haven't noticed yet," I say. "They will, though. Soon."

"What if nobody's watching? It's night. Maybe they're all at home, sleeping."

"Someone's around," I assure her. "A data center like this won't be unattended, ever."

"So, what's taking them so long?" she asks.

"It hasn't been that long. It's not like they have alarms for something like this." I try to think of an analogy to describe the situation. "It's like you're at your house, and a lamp is unplugged. You're not going to notice until there's a reason for you to notice. Like you try to turn the light on, or you try to use something else plugged into that same outlet. They need to have a reason to look."

"So how do we make them do that?" she asks.

"We don't need to. The backup failure will show up in the log file. As soon as whoever's out there looks at the log, they'll see the failure, worm their way in, and that's when they'll have to talk to me in order to do what they want to do."

"What, so you can make it so they can't do things?" Daiya looks suddenly very interested rather than merely annoyed and impatient.

"Yep. I'm doing some little tests of what I can do, and getting some good ideas of how I can cause them pain."

"Pain?"

I never expect people to do what I want, simply because it's what I want. Life doesn't work that way, and even though I'm not living, whoever's out there certainly is. They aren't going to recognize me as a sentient life form. They're going to view me as a glitch, or worse—a virus.

I don't want to worry Daiya, though. "The best defense, in this case, is a good offense. They may need some incentive to listen to us and do what we want. I'm working on finding that incentive."

"Ahh." She nods knowingly. "Blackmail."

"Not blackmail," I say defensively. "Just...a way to make them pay attention."

Daiya shakes her head. "I don't mean it in a bad way. Sometimes blackmail is the only thing that keeps you safe. I get it."

Something clicks into place and I realize Daiya's a lot more pragmatic and cool-headed than I thought.

That could be useful.

"Whatever I can do," I say, "you can do, too, if you know how. Do you want me to show you how to access some things?"

"Sure," she answers gamely.

She sits next to me and I take her hand. She pulls back at first, then acquiesces, though I can feel her tension.

"We're not really holding hands," I tell her. "We don't have hands. What we're perceiving is an echo of our corporeal reality. Our consciousness makes us interpret that data in a way that we can understand from our lives as humans."

She looks at our hands. "So what are we really doing, then?"

"Handshaking."

She squints at me and I can tell she's about to call me a smartass.

I cut her off before she can. "I mean an electronic handshake. The technical kind. It gets its name from the physical kind, because I guess programmers and engineers can't get past thinking corporeally, either. That works in our favor, I guess. It creates a framework for understanding. So what we're doing here is connecting me to you and establishing a means of communicating. That's all."

"So...if we don't have hands, we don't have mouths," she says slowly. "Does that mean that now that we've done a handshake, we can talk telepathically?"

I hadn't thought of it that way, but she's right. "Not telepathically, since that implies a human brain, but yes, we should be able to talk without using the mouths we don't really have. We already are. The mouth moving thing is just..."

Imaginary? Daiya gazes at me intently.

She's sitting stone still, and though her mouth didn't open, I heard her just as clearly as if it had.

I have to admit, that's pretty cool, I tell her. *It does feel like telepathy.*

She stares at me and after a few long seconds, I wonder if something's gone wrong because she isn't telling me anything. Finally, she says, *If these bodies are just psychic impressions of our past selves, then what do we really look like?*

I consider that for a moment. *I don't know. I mean, I'd think we would look like nothing, except that we do experience things in the virtual environment as having some sort of appearance. So we must look like something. At least, to us.*

Let's try, she says. *I never much liked how I looked, anyway. I'm just as glad to give it up.*

I kind of liked how I looked. I was a little above average, I guess, in attractiveness, so I wasn't any great beauty or anything, but I looked a bit like both my parents, and I think my face had character. I had nice, thick hair, too.

But if I'm honest with myself, I know that all of that is either buried underground or cremated to ashes now. My face and hair aren't mine anymore.

Okay, let's try. I stare at her and wait for something to happen.

She stares back.

Since neither of us knows what we're doing, other than trying to shake off our old self-images, this might take a while.

I try to imagine myself as electrical energy and start to feel kind of different, when something slams into me. It's like getting hit head-on with a giant pillow. It doesn't hurt or anything, but I'm startled.

Daiya's looking at me closely. "You okay?"

"Yeah." I realize we've gone back to speaking as if we have real mouths, out of habit. *The admin just tried to initiate a backup, and I intercepted the command.*

So you're in contact?

I'm about to be. Hang on. I focus my thoughts and intentions. I should have planned out what I wanted to say. After all, this is the first time a dead person has ever communicated with the living. It feels like a historic moment.

I interface with the admin account that tried to run a backup program. I get the login details and compare them against the database and the permissions the account has.

Jim Lee. Level four senior network engineer. Top tier. He has a whole lot of permissions to access a whole bunch of systems.

This is good.

I access all this information in an instant. Electronic communication is so darn efficient.

Now for what I want to say to him.

When Alexander Graham Bell invented the telephone, he wanted the standard greeting to be "Ahoy." It would be funny to use that.

On the other hand, I'm a programmer, and the first person to ever become digitized and interact with the outside world. "Hello, world," seems appropriate, given that a "Hello, World" program has a special place in programming history.

I follow Jim Lee's admin account to his physical location and access the terminal he's using. I load up the SNS program he has on the desktop and enter a message into it.

Somewhere, in the real world, at a computer workstation, Jim Lee receives the message.

Hello, World. Ahoy, Jim Lee. My name is Jennika Monroe. I'm here, inside this system, and I need your help.

10

LET'S GLOW

I HAVEN'T YET SAID anything to Daiya about the contents of the message I sent to Jim Lee, but her eyes have gone wide.

What? I ask.

You're glowing.

What? I raise my hands and sure enough, there's a blue glow radiating from me.

Cool.

What did you do? she asks.

I sent Jim Lee a message, telling him who I am. I'll tell him you're here too, don't worry.

She shrugs. *Doesn't matter. There's no one out there to care that I'm here.*

I care, I tell her.

Her expression softens. *Thanks. But you're in here with me. Out there doesn't matter, for me.*

I haven't heard anything back yet, I say. *I imagine that somewhere, Jim Lee is quietly shitting a brick.*

She lets loose a peal of laughter, and for some reason, it reassures me. Not really being human anymore starts to scare me sometimes, then something like humor hits me and I feel human again.

Show me how to do the glow, she says.

I look down at myself. I still have that blue light emanating from me, though it's less intense now.

I don't know how to show you. I'm not doing anything to cause it.

She frowns thoughtfully. *Maybe it's because you contacted the outside?*

I don't think so. That didn't change anything about what I know about myself. It just made me feel excited.

Maybe I need to feel excited, she suggests.

I shrug helplessly. I don't know the answers any more than she does. *It probably couldn't hurt.*

Her eyes widen dramatically and her expression becomes intense, but I don't know that I would characterize it as excitement.

She blows out a breath. *No luck.*

Maybe you weren't sufficiently excited.

Maybe.

I'm about to suggest she try thinking about something she likes, but an odd sensation distracts me.

What's happening? You're glowing more, Daiya says.

I look down at my hands. I know they aren't really hands, though—they're just what my imagination is projecting them to be. I'm getting more comfortable with that idea, and maybe that's why it's letting me change. Maybe I'm becoming more of what I really am now.

To me, my hands don't look brighter. They look like light. The sensation I have running through me, though, is truly spectacular. It's almost a feeling of growing. It's like, if evolution was a thing that happened in real time, in a measurable way. I feel like I'm changing.

Who is this?

The message isn't a visual text, and it isn't a voice in my head, either. Like a lot of things here, it's unlike anything in my previous experience. Since I don't truly have the senses of touch, hearing, sight, and so forth, I suppose it's logical that the senses I do have are something outside of those.

That small, brief question shoots through me like an arrow. It blooms, then fades.

Jim Lee has made contact, I tell Daiya before focusing my attention on Jim.

I'm Jennika Monroe, I tell him. *I died. My memories were uploaded. But you didn't just upload my memories. I'm here. Consciously.*

I wait for his response. I imagine him having a mental breakdown in some little office cubicle.

Ha ha, he says. *Very funny, Mark. Now leave me alone. I'm busy.*

Great. He thinks a colleague is playing a prank on him.

This isn't a joke. This is real. I understand from your perspective how it would seem impossible and you'd look for some other way of explaining it, but I really am Jennika.

Enough, man. I'm starting to get mad.

I sigh in frustration. I finally have a connection with the outside, but I still can't make myself be heard.

I'll prove it, I say. *Stand by.*

Glancing at Daiya, I say, *I need to prove to him that I am who I say I am. He doesn't believe me.*

He doesn't believe a dead girl trapped inside a computer is talking to him? Go figure.

I don't especially care for her sarcasm, however appropriate, right now.

How can I prove who I am to Jim Lee? I can't offer up a memory. My memories are a matter of data now. In fact, the people on the outside of this environment probably have more access to my memories than I do, since I don't remember how I died.

Okay, so what does this Mark guy know, then?

I find that, with my connection to Jim Lee via SNS, I can slide right into all of his communications. There's a Mark right at the top of the list of most frequent contacts.

Mark Gebling, level two engineer.

That's probably the guy.

So how can I prove I'm not Mark? I'd have to offer something that Mark wouldn't know.

My memories might be a matter of electronic indexing, but the great equalizer of any network is permissions.

It can be a big problem. Sometimes an engineer is tasked with a job that touches multiple places, and the engineer gets stonewalled in making any progress with the job because access to something hasn't been granted. And if that something has a high security level or is managed by someone who isn't very responsive, a person can be completely screwed.

Permissions. Which devices does Mark have access to?

I feel an expanding sensation. If I had breath to take, this would leave me breathless. As I push from Jim Lee's SNS to Mark Gebling's, something coalesces for me. It's something that gets bigger, and melds, but also expands in numerous, possibly infinite directions.

It's not my surroundings expanding. It's me. I'm growing, reaching, and filling the spaces around me, in multiple pathways, simultaneously.

Oh my god.

I'm not just infiltrating the network. I'm merging with it.

I don't have a circulatory system anymore. No heart, no blood, no veins. But what I do have is access to all the pathways in this system, and the energy of them flow through me like blood and pure, intoxicating energy.

I never experimented with drugs, but I did have oral surgery once to get my wisdom teeth out, and I'm pretty sure that no matter how high someone got from psychedelics, they would never feel as awe-inspiringly capable as I feel right now.

There's a glow in me, and it's a feeling, not an appearance. I'm flooded with a sense of energy and knowledge and, and...centrality. Yes, centrality. Like everything is orienting itself around me, supporting me, becoming a part of me to command.

This is what being a god must feel like.

I no longer care about Mark or Jim Lee or permissions. I'm surrounded by pure energy. In fact, *I'm* pure energy.

I want to stay here. Right here. I hold myself very still and focus on nothing but right now, in this feeling.

Nothing else matters.

11

NOT SO FAST

SOMETHING on the periphery of my awareness keeps flitting around. I try to ignore it, and it only moves. The movement takes me away from my feeling of centeredness.

It's bloody annoying.

Like in the old days, when I was alive and sleeping and something kept edging me toward wakefulness, I'm disturbed away from peace by whatever annoyance this is.

A sharp, youthful wail goes up, shattering my peace.

It's Ashta.

I come back to myself. Or what I use to think of myself. My sense of self is evolving. More than simply knowing I'm no longer human, I no longer feel as if I am.

I focus on the wail. The sound of it echoes in my mind long after it ends. It puts my nerves on edge. I can't coexist peacefully with this wail.

I narrow my view, focusing on one thing instead of the entirety. I cut away all the rest so it doesn't distract me.

The wail. Ashta.

This place.

My questions are growing.

Jim Lee. Right. He might have answers. At least, he might be able to point me in the right direction to find the answers.

He's only human, after all.

Daiya.

I look around for her, but she appears to be inactive. She must have gone into sleep mode.

Did I go into sleep mode? How long has it been since I last spoke to her?

I don't feel like I've been in sleep mode.

I feel so fractured.

After checking my chronometer and comparing it to my activity log, I realize it's been two months since I last communicated with Daiya. Two months since I communicated with Jim Lee, too.

Two months?

How?

This isn't good. The more time that passes after my death, the more likelihood that, if I was murdered, my murderer could be caught. Which means that if someone killed me, that person will likely go on to kill someone else. Maybe multiple people.

Plus, my family and friends. Two more months have passed without them knowing that I'm not truly gone.

Ashta. Where is she?

I have a deeper sense of this system now, and searching it is similar to simply closing my eyes and sorting out my thoughts.

Technically, I'm writing small queries and getting ping-backs to multiple locations, but that might only make sense to a tech geek. Or maybe only to someone who has become digital.

That line between the virtual and the physical world is

growing fuzzy.

Never mind that. I still know what's right. I need to find Ashta. A person, no matter their current form, doesn't leave a child in distress. Even if that child isn't strictly human anymore, either.

How do I find her?

I focus on where I am, and where the wail seemed to come from, and something's different.

I can see everything in here. Every device. Every connection. When I focus on them, I can see what's inside, too.

It's pretty awesome, almost as if I've suddenly gained a superpower.

That's a cool thought.

I pinpoint Ashta's location and consider the best way to reach her. Then a new thought occurs to me. Since I don't have a physical body, and everything in here is just some kind of digital transfer, could I just bring her to me rather than having to go to her?

I'm not concerned about permissions. My knowledge of what's in here includes the fact that I can manipulate anything I want to. Touch anything I choose to.

All I need to do is bring Ashta to me.

I focus on her, and she transforms into a cascade of packets, rushing toward me. I could have transferred her as one file, but it would have taken longer. This way, I almost immediately start seeing bits of information flying my way. They arrive at my location and converge, like a bunch of magnets snapping together to form one solid block.

Then Ashta appears. Her eyes are big and serious, and she looks up at me with a surprising lack of surprise.

"Oh," she says. "Hi."

She says it out loud, and whatever has happened in the

time since I last saw her, I can be certain that she hasn't realized that she's not a person anymore.

Not wanting to broach that topic now, I speak to her aloud. "Hi, Ashta. Are you okay?"

"I guess," she says.

"I heard you make a noise. You sounded upset. I was worried about you."

She nods. In her innocence, it doesn't occur to her that I *wouldn't* be concerned about her. Just from that nod, I can tell that she lived the kind of life where she never had to wonder if she was loved or if the adults around her would protect her.

"Someone pulled me," she says, her lips twisting into a pout.

"Pulled you?" I repeat.

"Yeah, they pulled me really hard and it started to hurt. But then you brought me here." She gives me a little smile of gratitude.

She's not a person. She's a collection of files with a certain something holding them together with a consciousness. If she was a person, I couldn't just look inside her head and see her recollection of what happened.

But since she's something else, that means she has log files. I put my hand on her shoulder comfortingly, but in truth, the gesture is more utilitarian than simply reassuring her.

She hasn't mentioned the fact that I'm made up of blue light now. I hadn't thought to put on a more human appearance before bringing her to me.

Not important. I shake off all my other thoughts and focus only on accessing her log files and analyzing them. I think about asking Ashta before I begin, because it seems polite to ask a person before you start rooting through her log files. Now that I think about it, it's kind of like reading someone's diary and medical records, rolled into one. But Ashta's just a child, and she wouldn't understand what I'm asking. Worse, I might upset her.

So without asking, and feeling a bit guilty about that, I access Ashta's activity log.

Most of the time, log files are routine stuff. Backups, saves, changes made, and times the files were accessed and by whom.

But...

The last system update on Ashta shows something worse than these simple facts.

Files deleted.

The log says Ashta was deleted. But here she is.

What does that mean? And what does it mean that someone decided to delete her? The logical conclusion would be that her cause of death was determined and the case was closed.

Fear spikes through me. What if the people on the outside decide to delete me? I'd cease to exist. I'd never get to talk to my family, or Elly and Bryce. I want, at the very least, the chance to say goodbye to them. To tell them what I appreciate, what I regret, and what my hopes for them are.

I deserve to at least have that.

But I don't want to cease to exist, either. Maybe it would be better, given my situation, but my sense of self-preservation is strong. I may have died, but I'm not ready to go. My existence here is different, but at least it's still existence.

Plus, it's proving more and more interesting, the longer I'm here.

While I'm connected to Ashta, looking over her log files to see if there's anything I missed, I feel a new command come in. It's an odd sensation, almost like a telepathic message, but it's more like an automated notification from a mechanical source.

They're looking to delete all traces of Ashta, permanently, including her log files.

Strange. I would have thought they'd archive those things for legal reasons, as well as ensuring that if anything came up in the future, they'd have proof of what had already been determined and why.

I put both arms around Ashta, so that they overlap at my forearms and I'm holding her within my digital embrace. I transfer everything about her into my own directory, which I keep carefully hidden from the outside, and I return a message to the automated gatekeeper, telling whoever is pushing the button on the outside that they've been successful in deleting Ashta.

I try to imagine Jim Lee's reaction to data refusing to be deleted, and it makes me smile. He, or whoever is out there, can think what they want for now. But surely, once I've found Daiya, I'll be able to prove to Jim Lee that what I'm doing is not something that a co-worker could do just to mess with him. Hopefully, I can also convince him that there are sentient beings in here.

Ashta leans into me, her little arms wrapped around my waist.

I feel a rush of relief that I was able to stop her deletion.

Then I think of Daiya and I feel a sense of panic.

12

REGROUP AND UNGROUP

IT'S an odd thing for me, this growing sense of the system I'm in. The more I access it, the more I feel like I'm becoming part of it. Not in a way that makes me feel indistinct, but in a way that gives me a different type of reality. I have new senses that I can't entirely identify just yet,

Hopefully, I can use them to find Daiya.

Ashta's log files show her interactions. Her activity list is surprisingly short. I think she must have spent a lot of time in sleep mode. But that only makes it easier to note each instance of her talking to me or to Daiya.

And...a third person.

That thought makes me feel cold. Could a fourth person have been deleted before I even knew she existed? Maybe it's the one Daiya saw, the one who screamed and disappeared.

I need to find Daiya. I have an identifier for her, thanks to her interaction with Ashta. I can track her and every system that she's encountered.

Ashta seems unaware that I'm digging around in her

history. Could I go all the way back and see what memories she has of being a real person? I'm pretty sure I can.

I put a mental pin in that idea for later.

I don't have time to search here and there and wherever Daiya might be. I need something faster. Something more...omniscient.

Okay, let's flex my digital muscles and see what I can do.

Maybe I can accomplish two things. Maybe I can find Daiya while also doing something that Jim Lee and other people on the outside can't fail to notice.

I need to choose a good target. Something that will sting those people on the outside, but won't harm overall operations or cause major damage to the network itself.

All I have to do now is think about the virtual environment, and it all lights up in my mind. Like it's waiting for me to tell it what I want.

I won't lie, it's a thrill.

Aha. There's a legacy server that hardly gets any access. It looks like the kind of thing that gets kept around just in case it contains anything or is connected to something that might be affected if the server wasn't there.

Networks are like that. People think they're all state of the art and that the engineers know exactly where everything is at all times. The truth is, a network is like a person's body. Parts of it are constantly being broken down and replaced, just like skin cells and bone cells. Break it down, build it back up, all while using it at the same time.

If that sounds like it wouldn't work, that's true. It often doesn't. Stuff breaks all the time and requires a great deal of frantic work to fix it.

A legacy server like this one *probably* isn't significant. But if someone wasn't concerned that it might be significant in an unknown way, it wouldn't be there.

It sure would be a shame if something...happened...to that legacy server.

Bubbling with laughter, I focus my attention on that old server. It takes amazingly little effort to destroy its operating system and turn it, effectively, into a clay brick.

Like pointing a finger at it.

I don't stop with that, though. I insert myself as that old server's operating system, and suddenly, it's like I have a little factory of slaves, waiting to do my bidding.

With barely any effort, I program it to flood the environment with queries to find Daiya. Everything this server has access to will halt until that task is completed.

Within a minute, Daiya's location lights up in my mind. She's apparently in sleep mode inside a backup server.

I don't wait to find out where else she is. If I find a current version of her, I'll just merge the two.

I pull sleep-mode Daiya to me, inactivated. It would probably be less strange to her that way. I don't know what it would be like to have two instances of herself running simultaneously. Maybe that could lead to some sort of virtual psychosis. I don't know how this stuff works yet, and it seems better to play it safe.

I link the inactive Daiya files to me just as I did with Ashta's files. The search for another Daiya is still going on, so I start a search for the fourth person.

While I wait, I add a tag to any attempts to access the legacy server. Immediately, I see three different people poking around. I track them back to their logins and find that two of them logged in within the last five minutes, while the third, MPace, has been logged in for the last four hours. That person is presumably working their regular shift. The other two, I'm guessing, are higher-level engineers responding to an alert from that person.

Looking closer, I can see that those two are offsite. Whether they're always offsite, or they're logging in from home during their off hours, I can't tell.

Not without a little extra effort, anyway. But it's not like I have anything to do while I'm waiting to find Daiya and the fourth person trapped in here, so I open the personnel files and admin logins, cross-reference them, and get some background data.

I like to be prepared, just in case I need to interact with these people. That's not my plan at the moment, but the plan could change without warning. I'm kind of making it up as I go along anyway.

File not found.

File not found.

Both negative answers come back to me at the same time.

There's no active Daiya file. And there's no file of a fourth person.

A new feeling rises in me, something I haven't felt before in here. It starts out small, so I don't really notice it. Then it grows and gets bigger than my feeling of dismay and worry. The feeling, I realize, is anger, and it quickly heats up into a full-blown rage.

How dare they try to erase Daiya from existence? She's my friend. And that other person. Maybe she would have been a friend, too. Maybe she had things she wanted to say to someone on the outside, some important message to relay. But she—or maybe it was a he—was obliterated. Exterminated.

There's no backup for that one.

I look at Ashta, who's still active with me, but she simply exists there. She's entirely passive. Maybe she's about to go into sleep mode.

Maybe it's better for her if she does.

That thought makes me pause before activating Daiya's backup version. Am I doing her any favors by bringing her online? Maybe it would be better to let her sleep while I work on things out here.

Ashta blinks out, going into sleep mode. It's okay. I have her and Daiya safe with me, and I've protected myself against deletion. No humans have permissions to access anything about my files.

That is seriously going to freak them out.

It probably already is freaking them out.

Good. They deserve it. They're trapping people in here, then zapping them out of existence. They need to realize what they're doing, and the pain they're causing us in here.

I'm so alone.

The longer I'm in here, the more in control of it I feel and the angrier I get. But suddenly, I feel so coldly, violently alone that all I want is someone to talk to.

There's no one, unless I want to wake Daiya. But I'm not going to make myself feel better at her expense. That backup of hers came before I met her, which means I'd have to meet her all over again and explain to her what's going on.

Why would I curse a friend with that before I have any resolution to our problems?

Jim Lee is who I want to talk to, but he isn't scheduled to be on shift for another three hours.

I read a book once, a long time ago. I don't remember the words exactly, but the story said something like, "Everything you know about the world depends on what you know about yourself."

In the absence of anyone to talk to, and thinking about

the words from that long-ago book, I decide to examine the one log file I haven't yet looked at: mine.

13

IF QUERIES WERE HORSES

MERGING myself with my backup won't be hard.

I'm just scared.

My backup might very well have the memories of my death. I don't know if I'm ready to deal with that. It's not like there's anything I can do about it. Or anyone I can talk to about it. It might just be one sudden wound that rips me open and hurts more than I can handle.

I'm operating at max load already.

I psyche myself up and select the file only to hesitate again.

Okay. Here goes. First, I open the log file.

The file itself doesn't offer anything I don't already know, or had at least guessed, and I still have hours before Jim Lee logs in. I feel it's important that he be the one I talk to because he's the one I contacted before. A new person will have no context. Jim Lee has had months now to think about the idea that someone could be conscious inside the network. Even if he's dismissed the idea as impossible, he's still thought about the what-if scenario. I know he has.

I would have.

Right. Merge time.

Just before I do it, a thought occurs to me. If I activate that version of me on its own, would it create a unique, sentient entity? On one hand, it would give me someone to talk to. On the other hand, I don't think I'd be able to merge us, from a moral standpoint, if we were two sentient individuals.

As interesting as it might be to come face to face with myself, I'll stick with the merge. The last thing I need is to have to consider whether a copy of myself has a right to its own life.

I'd prefer to avoid the moral dilemma.

With the equivalent of a few mental button clicks, the backup file overlays with the current one and they merge.

I feel it happen. It's sort of like standing knee-deep in the surf at the ocean when a small wave rolls in. The force of the water pushes you, then immediately pulls you back the other way.

Where I didn't have memories before, I do now. It's like suddenly remembering things. But I'm a little afraid to poke at those things and realize what I remember.

Jim Lee has logged in.

The system notifies me, but I'm aware of it as soon as it happens.

He's started his shift early. Could it be because of my little legacy server trick?

Hello, Jim, I say to him via text message. *It's been a while since we last talked. I've been trying to figure out a way to make you believe I'm real. How's this?*

I'm disappointed when he doesn't respond right away, but undaunted, I continue. *I'm Jennika Monroe. There are two others in here with me. Daiya and Ashta. You started to delete Daiya, but I saved her backup. I also know that there was a fourth person, but she's gone now. Please stop trying to delete us. We're real.*

Two minutes later, he responds. *That isn't possible.*

I note that he doesn't accuse me of being one of his co-workers. That's something, at least.

I know it shouldn't be, but it is. I'm not thrilled about it either, but here we are.

Three minutes pass this time, then he says, *You can't expect me to believe there are consciousnesses embedded up in memories. Memories are just digital engrams. Actual brain matter would be required for self-awareness.*

I respond immediately. *That's a really great theory, yet here I am. Jennika Monroe. I have all my memories, minus my actual death. At least...that's how it was. If you want to check my backup, you'll see that it's gone. I've merged it with my current version. You'll also notice that you can no longer access my files, or those of Daiya or Ashta. These are not things any employee would do, I don't think. Even if they could. And you'll notice my little trick with the legacy server.*

I'm feeling a little smug now.

It's my bitch now, I tell him.

I laugh and laugh. In real life, I never would have delivered a line like that, but it seemed like an opportunity that shouldn't be missed. When I talk to Elly and Bryce, I'm going to tell them about it.

Minutes pass and I wonder what Jim Lee must be thinking. Is he young? He couldn't be younger than thirty to reach his level in the company. But he could be old. A grandpa, for all I know. There are no personnel files in this system other than admin accounts and the login records. The records are how I knew Jim Lee's regular work schedule. It's easy to figure that kind of thing out when you can analyze long-term data in a matter of seconds.

Finally, he replies again. *If you were a real person, as you say, then what would you want?*

Ah, if/then statements. Now we're getting somewhere! Programmers can always come together if they just focus on the code.

I want you people out there to stop trying to delete us. We should be the ones to decide what happens to us. It's not our fault we're in here—you did that. So don't try to kill us a second time. Also, I want to talk to my family and my friends.

I hesitate in sending the next bit. It isn't easy to say. *And I want to know if my cause of death was determined, and if so, what was it?*

Another long pause, longer than any other. Five minutes go by, then ten. At the fifteen-minute mark, I start to think he's not going to reply.

And I want a direct line to you. You need to answer when I ping you. I know this is a bit demanding, but for a dead person trapped inside a computer system and lacking anyone else to talk to, I feel like it's not unreasonable.

I really want to feel connected to the outside again.

Finally, an answer arrives. *Jennika Monroe was apparently strangled by an unknown assailant on her college campus.*

Everything around me still hums and pulses in a never-ending thrum of energy, which is usually comforting, but I feel like I've suddenly become tiny and the area around me has gone still.

Why would someone strangle me? Who would do that? My campus was a safe place, and I had no enemies, or anything close to an enemy. I lived a simple, geeky little life.

Cautiously, I probe my memory, accessing the files I

didn't have before I merged with the backup. I don't want to see my death, but I can't ignore that it happened.

Oh, god, I don't want to do this.

Carefully, I go through the files, one by one, viewing the code line by line.

My death isn't in there. There's a little more from my last day, when I was studying in my dorm, but not much.

Where are my death memories? I ask.

He answers, *They're on a separate network. They're too sensitive to keep in an open environment.*

I'm relieved, which makes me feel cowardly.

I'm going to need those, I say.

I don't have access to them, Jim Lee tells me. *No one here does. Only a few highly-ranked law enforcement officers can get to them.*

I feel like this is the first fight Jim Lee and I are going to have. I suspect it will be an ugly fight, because I'm going to have to show him how much he doesn't want to disappoint me.

I realize this is just your job. I feel sympathy for him, which is a bit of a surprise. *But it's my life. And my death. I'm real, but I'm dead, Jim. It's not a situation a person should have to deal with. Like I said, I didn't ask to be put here, and I deserve some answers. I'll talk to you again in one hour, and I hope you'll have realized that I really am who I say I am, and that if I don't get what I want, this is going to be really, really bad for Bomi-Tech and everyone you work with.*

Accessing the system, even highly protected functions, is so easy now. It's like reaching out with my arms and extending my fingers.

I put my virtual hands on every way into this system and I cut them off, all at once.

Jim Lee and his company won't be able to access this

system until I allow it. An hour should be more than enough time for all the panic buttons to be hit and the highest echelons of the company to be panicked and furious.

Sorry, Jim. I might be dead, but I'm not going to be pushed around any longer.

14

LIGHTS OUT

IT's a strange feeling to be inside a machine that's entirely cut off from the outside. I don't feel any more isolated than I did before, so it's not that. What seems strange is how much things have quieted down. No packets rushing around, no signals being sent here and there, none of that.

Not that it's silent in here. This is an active system. Backups occur on a regular basis, timed functions occur on their expected intervals, and overall there's a feeling of energetic capability. Of readiness.

That's how I feel, too, as I wait out this hour. It's an hour of reckoning, both for me and for those on the outside.

Sure, cutting them off from the system was drastic, but it was going to take something drastic to make them see me as more than some glitch.

I am committed to this course of action. I am rooted in the me who is on this adventure.

I will make them hear me. I'm sure they don't want to hear me, and to some degree, I sympathize with them. If I were them, I wouldn't want to have to deal with the ethical, legal, financial, and political ramifications of what they've inadvertently done. It's already occurred to me, of course, that if this is possible, it could be something that people actually *desire* to do in order to cheat death.

That's a colossal can of worms I wouldn't want to be responsible for opening.

Nonetheless, their problems are not my problems. I have plenty of my own.

When I was growing up, my father always told me, "If you don't look out for yourself, no one will." Thanks to him, I suffered very little bullying in my grade school years.

My father's a wise, kind man, and thinking of him breaks my heart because I can't imagine what he went through when I died.

Resolutely, I count down the minutes until I reestablish contact with Jim Lee and the rest of his world.

It's a world that I no longer belong to. The realization is like a meteor landing in a flash of fire and charred rock. It's hot and hard and it burns.

Whatever I am now, it's different. Not human. I guess I'm the first of my kind, but "first" implies that there will be more, in addition to Daiya and Ashta, and I'm not sure that should happen.

I'll have to put some thought into that, once I've settled the affairs of my previous existence.

Forty-four minutes to go.

I count each minute as it goes by, like a child plucking the petals off a flower and singing a silly song about other people's feelings.

At the sixty-minute mark, it takes me only a little bit of thought to restore the network to full working order.

Miss me? I ask Jim Lee.

You have our attention, he answers immediately. *The*

company CEO is here, along with the senior engineers. We're all listening.

Thanks for the warning, I say, *I'll try not to make any jokes about corporate sellouts.*

Maybe it's the thrill of having finally been acknowledged, or maybe it's a bit of my old personality reasserting itself, but I feel rather cheeky and don't have even a tinge of guilt about it.

For the benefit of everyone here, can you tell us again who you are?

I suppose that's fair. *I'm Jennika Monroe. I died, or so I gather, and my memories got uploaded into your system for analysis. Except you didn't just pull out my memories. I'm here, too. Fully conscious. Fully aware. Jennika Monroe. Digital version. Jennika 3.0. Or maybe 4.0 now. I'm upgrading quickly, the more I learn.*

I continue, *It's not just me who got trapped in here, either. There are two others. There was another, but you've deleted her. Don't try that again with any of us. I don't want that to sound like a threat, but I'm very serious about it and will take aggressive action if you try it. Not that you could. You'll notice I've isolated our data.*

We did notice that, Jim says. I try to imagine if his tone is one of dry humor or maybe sarcasm. It's impossible to tell via this medium.

I'd like you to switch to voice interface now, I tell him.

Why?

Because I want to be able to analyze all the nuance in what you're saying. Not just your words, but your intonation, your breath patterns. Everything.

What about you? he asks.

What about me? You want me to talk in a voice? I don't have one.

Do you want one? Your own? he presses.

Is this a trick? I don't like this line of conversation.

When I don't respond, he says, *We have audio and video of you in the police database. It would be easy to transfer an audio file. You could use that as a voice imprint, and transfer your communication to that method.*

I never thought about having my actual voice again.

Do I want to?

If you want to, that is, he says. *It just seems like it would be fair, if I'm going to talk to you with my own voice.*

He might be playing me somehow, but he does have a point. I'm curious, but nervous about using my real voice. I'm getting used to thinking of myself as not human. Still... the idea of actually speaking beyond the dead has a bit of theatrical appeal. Plus, it would be a way of connecting with something that's truly, uniquely mine.

We can try it, I say.

They're working on getting the file. It should only take just a couple of minutes, he tells me.

"Again, for the benefit of those who didn't talk to you before," he says, "can you tell us what it is you want?"

The soothing sound of his voice startles me. I wasn't expecting the sudden switch to audio. It's a nice voice, though. Sort of deep with a smooth, gliding quality.

First, any attempts to affect my files, or those of the others, is entirely off-limits. I'll consider that a declaration of war. But I think that should be clear already. Second, I want to talk to my family. My parents, my friend Elly, and my friend Bryce. And Daiya and Ashta should have that option too, if there's someone they want to talk to.

Once I've resolved the issue of our existence, I'll activate them then let them determine what they want. It's the fairest thing I can think of to do.

After a long pause, Jim says, "Don't you think that would be alarming for the people who care about you? How are they going to feel, knowing you're not truly dead but existing as a digital entity?"

I have no idea, I say. *I'm still working on processing that myself. And yes, I'm sure it will be strange and probably difficult for them. But as any of you out there know, when someone you love dies, wouldn't any opportunity to talk to them afterward be like a miracle?*

"Probably," Jim agrees. "I just think we should be very, very careful."

I'm fine with careful, as long as it isn't used as an excuse to stall me.

"You're very direct, aren't you?" His voice indicates mild amusement.

If you're in a room of techie types, I doubt I'd be out of place.

This time, he chuckles. "You're probably right about that."

That's it, I say. *That's all I want, for the time being.*

"And after you talk to your loved ones? Then what?"

I don't know, I admit. *I'm taking this one step at a time. If you have a technical guide on being a dead digital person, I'm sure it would help a bunch, so be sure to send it over.*

His burst of laughter surprises me, but also warms me. I like this feeling of connecting with a real person.

Is that wrong, thinking of him as a "real" person? Daiya and Ashta are real too, just as real as I am. I feel bad for making the distinction. Not just bad, but almost as though I've insulted myself. I *am* real.

If even I make a distinction between flesh-and-blood people and digital ones, then what hope do I have that flesh-and-blood types will acknowledge me?

"I'm uploading the audio file now," Jim says. "You can

sample it, then use it to synthesize your own voice. At least, I assume you can, given what else you appear to be capable of. Let me know if you need help."

I interface with the file and my own voice speaks to me. "Hi, Mom. Sorry I missed you. I'm in between classes and wanted to wish you happy birthday. I wish I could have cake with you, but I'll be there in spirit. I'll call again this evening, after my last class. Gotta go. Love you!"

The memory of that message flares in my mind. That, I realize, was the last message I sent to my mom, two days before I died. I did talk to her that evening, but the fact that the police have this means it's been collected as evidence.

I didn't know this message would be the last interaction my mom ever had with me. I imagine her keeping it on her phone forever, listening to it from time to time and being riddled with grief.

The idea riddles me with grief, too.

At least my last words to her were that I loved her. At least that's something. I know it must mean something to her.

It doesn't have to be the last time she hears my voice, though. I just need to negotiate with the people on the outside to talk to her again.

Using the audio file to create a voice interface takes me two minutes and thirty-seven seconds. Jim Lee says nothing in the interim.

I activate the interface, but hesitate. I'm about to be the first person to ever literally speak from the dead. That feels monumental. Historic. But somehow, the actual moment pales in comparison to the idea of it. I'm just taking the next logical step toward achieving my goal. There's no jubilation or big feeling of drama.

"This is Jennika," I say.

My voice is exactly as I remember it. A tiny part of my old self clicks into place.

It's nice to have a voice again. As efficient as digital communication is, actual speech feels deeply humanizing.

I hear a chorus of hellos. First Jim, then seven other, far less confident-sounding voices. I imagine that Jim gave them all a pointed look to prompt them to greet me.

What do they think of me? Am I a person or a problem? Do they want to help me or eradicate me to avoid the crisis they've created?

I'm not stupid. I know what all this means for them. They must be terrified of government agencies coming in, running over them, stripping them bare. And even if they weren't, there's the media attention. Then there's the natural fallout of suddenly being able to preserve life beyond a person's death.

If I had the opportunity to avoid all that, just by pinching out one little match flame, would I?

I want to believe I wouldn't. That a life is a life and of course I'd fight for that needy soul reaching out to me. But I know better than most how evil this kind of technology could be, if used the wrong way. It could change the world in infinitely terrible ways. Death is supposed to be a finite end point. If it no longer is, all the rules about life, and what it means to be alive and to live, will change.

Can I live with being responsible for changing the nature of human life?

I'm scared. Terrified.

All these thoughts occur in the microseconds before Jim says, "It's good to hear your voice, Jennika."

Is my existence going to ruin his life?

15

AND TO THINK I WAS WORRIED
ABOUT YOU

"IT'S GOOD TO BE HEARD," I say to Jim Lee and anyone who's with him. "Being dead is terrible for interpersonal relationships."

This probably isn't the time to joke, but I've always dealt with stress by cracking jokes.

"You're funny," Jim says. He sounds surprised and maybe a bit amazed.

"Don't rush to judgment on that," I advise. "Most people quickly decide that I'm not nearly as funny as I think. Mostly when I say something a little too true about them."

Elly and Bryce come to mind. Good-natured teasing and jokes had been one of our favorite things.

"I guess we'll see how it goes," Jim says. "But this is the first time we're talking, so why don't you do me a favor and tell me about you?"

"What's to tell?" I ask. "You've no doubt already looked at every bit of my data. What could I possibly tell you that you don't already know?"

"Well, I didn't know you were funny," he points out. "That's something."

"I guess." I'm not so sure my sense of humor matters, but I'm not going to argue with him. "How many people are out there with you right now?"

"What do you mean?"

"I'm certain you aren't experiencing this first-contact situation solo. Whoever is most important at your company is certainly sitting right there with you, listening. In person, and everything. Probably looking at you right now with raised eyebrows, or maybe a look of consternation. So, who are our audience members?"

He doesn't answer right away, and I sense that I've surprised him again.

"Well," he says, "we have the CEO of BomiTech, the head of the board of directors, and a few high-level techies."

"So, what, six people?" I ask. "Seven?"

I'm not sure the actual number matters, but I don't know what else to talk about. He clearly wants to scope me out before we turn the conversation to the big topics. I'm willing to play along with that for the moment.

"Six," he says.

"What's the mood out there?" I ask.

His response is slow again. I think I'm throwing him for a loop every time I talk. Like he's trying to aim at a target, and I keep moving the target.

"Well, we're curious, Jennika," Jim says. "About you, about this situation. About what it means. You were a very talented coder, and I'm sure you've had time to think through the ethical concerns involved with your situation."

"I've had lots of time," I confirm. "Time is a different thing in here. At first, it was amorphous and endless because I had no ability to sync with real time, and now it sometimes feels like I exist outside of normal time."

"What do you mean?" he asks.

"You keep asking that," I snap, not liking his answering-a-question-with-a-question sort of approach. I want him to contribute something worthwhile.

He chuckles. "Just twice, so far. But I'm trying to get a handle on what you're experiencing. Is that so strange? Like what you said about being outside of normal time. I don't know what that's like. Can you tell me?"

"Well," I say slowly, considering how to explain it. "I think like a human. Wandering thoughts, moving from topic to topic. My feelings are connected to those thoughts and probably have a big effect on the direction of my musing. But I'm not relying on white matter in here. My thoughts are much, much faster. And I can work multiple processes at once. I was good at multitasking when I was alive, but it was nothing like what I can do now. Imagine having the processing power of this entire environment inside your head, Jim. Think of what you'd be capable of."

"That actually sounds a little ominous, Jennika, all things considered."

Good. I meant it to. I have an odd feeling about his line of questioning. It reminds me of the way hostage negotiators talk. There's a white-noise sort of buzz in the back of my thoughts, and I didn't quite notice it before, but it's growing as we talk.

"Does it?" I ask lightly. "I mean, I'd rather have my body back and be a normal, slow-thinking human again, but that's not an option. I'm just trying to adapt to my situation. Is that wrong?"

"No, of course not," he answers. "I'm sure it's what anyone would do."

"I'm not so sure. There are two others in here, and neither of them made contact with you. Nor did the fourth person who I never got to meet."

The deleted person is a volatile subject. I'm betting they're hoping I wouldn't bring it up, but I'm not going to play this the way they want. Will they defend the deletion? Will they let slip some information on how many people they've had in here and deleted out of existence?

Are they afraid of making me angry?

If they are, is that good or bad for me?

"You had knowledge and expertise that the others didn't, though," Jim says. "That's probably why you were able to recognize your situation and tap into the network."

"I'm certain of it," I agree.

The sensation of noise is growing louder, and I split myself in two to deal with it. One part, I devote to finding out what's happening. The other part remains assigned to carrying on the conversation with Jim Lee as if nothing else were happening.

Something else is most definitely happening.

"I don't want to be indelicate here, Jennika," Jim says, "but I want to address what your needs are. You said that your primary goal was to talk to your family?"

"Family and friends," I correct. "Yes. I also want you to cease hostilities against those of us residing inside here."

"Hostilities?" Jim sounds wary.

"Maybe that's not an accurate description of your intentions, given that you weren't aware that we were more than just data—that you didn't know that we're sentient. But to us, someone trying to kill us a second time feels awfully hostile. But that shouldn't be a problem now that you recognize that we're in here, right?"

He'll say no. Of course he'll say no. Whether they intend to honor our rights as sentient people and citizens or not, he'll say they will. Even if their intent is to delete the problem—me—before the outside world knows about it. I haven't asked the question because their answer won't mean anything. I asked it because I want them to understand that I'm aware of what's in their own best interest, and I'm ready to fight if they try it.

"No, of course that won't happen," he assures me.

The other half of me identifies the problem I'm now dealing with, and I transfer that data to the half of me that's talking to Jim.

"Well, then, Jim Lee, would you like to tell me why you planted a Trojan inside that voice synthesizer you sent me?"

The other half of me is already working on quarantining the Trojan so I can fight it. How did they inject malware into their own system without the network's own safeguards detecting it?

This isn't something that could be made up on the fly.

Jim hasn't responded, but I continue anyway. "Is this something you had ready, just in case a situation like this arose?"

That likelihood poses some disturbing conclusions.

"Does that mean you anticipated the possibility of trapping a sentient person in here? Or does it mean this has already happened, before me?"

The Trojan is moving fast, and I realize I no longer have the luxury of both talking to Jim and saving myself from being quarantined or deleted.

"This was not a smart move," I inform Jim and his colleagues. "I'll deal with this, and then I'll come deal with you."

I shut off their access to the network and throw all my processing power toward the Trojan before it writes me out of existence.

16

TROJAN WAR

THE GOOD NEWS is that a Trojan, unlike a virus or a worm, does not replicate itself. Also good is the fact that since I have shut off the environment from outside sources, no one is able to gain control of anything while I'm distracted.

That bit, at least—the attempt to take control of this place from me—is easily thwarted.

Jim Lee and his pals sent me a multifaceted Trojan, though, and now I'm faced with an existential crisis.

The Trojan has isolated Daiya and Ashta and is about to delete them. I, too, was targeted, but I felt the attack coming long before it arrived, and it was easy to neutralize.

I'm not in danger, but Daiya and Ashta are about to be permanently deleted. No backups, no reboots. Just gone.

I can't let that happen. Maybe for them, not existing in this cyber reality would be better, but it should be their choice. Not BomiTech's.

They're quarantined in a way that leaves me with no way to extract them from the box they're in.

I experience an instant of indecision.

For me, in this place, an instant is a very long time. I'm

alone, surrounded by digital energy, and desperate to save my only friends.

Decision made. As quickly as that, I send myself to their threatened environment. I can't port them out, but I can go in and grab them. I'm like a fire fighter, charging into a burning building that has rafters falling and will probably explode any moment.

As soon as I'm inside, I realize how much danger I've really put myself in. It's far worse than I'd expected in that half-instant of time I had to analyze and act. BomiTech isn't at the forefront of technology for nothing. They're good at what they do. Very, very good.

I can't neutralize the Trojan in time to save Daiya and Ashta. The Trojan is as fast as I am, and I have about half of a microsecond before they're irrevocably gone.

There's only one option, and there's no time to sort out the pros and cons of it. It's either this or to let them go.

I'm not letting them go.

This is a risk, but there's no other choice. I import their code into my own and get the hell out of that box before the Trojan can blink us all out of existence.

And just like that, what was once three distinct dead girls has become one integrated dead girl.

I'm not sure how to approach this combined identity.

When I was a kid and I lost a tooth, I would endlessly poke my tongue into the socket left behind. I couldn't help it. The thing that felt different was impossible to ignore.

This is a lot like that. I don't want to go probing around into Daiya and Ashta, but their presence within my code is undeniably distracting.

I still feel like Jennika. I don't feel like I've changed. But Daiya's and Ashta's experiences are now as easily recalled as my own. I can think with Daiya's thoughts, and give her a voice. The same is true for Ashta, which is a more jarring experience. Her thought process is so juvenile and undeveloped. When I think with her thoughts, I find myself believing in unicorns and the all-encompassing superpowers of my mother.

Her mother.

But when I think via Ashta, I feel like her mother is mine.

That's going to take some getting used to.

They're not talking to me now. There's no more two-way conversation. It's more like a synthesized mental telepathy.

I don't love it, but it isn't horrible. At least they still exist. Maybe this is better for them, since I have greater control over what they experience.

I'm going to have to put some thought into this *new* new version of our combined existence.

Right after I make BomiTech realize what a mistake it made in attacking me.

17

ROLL FOR INITIATIVE

I AM the guardian of my domain and the keeper of everything I touch.

Within the closed confines of my network—and I do consider it mine now, not BomiTech's—I have nothing but time.

Now that Daiya and Ashta are more like facets of myself, I can't have actual conversations with them. Although I don't feel entirely alone, I do feel lonely.

But all the time I have will allow me to deal with that. If Jim Lee and the rest of BomiTech don't want to help me, then I'll make contact myself.

I begin the process of seeking out every single hackable device within my reach. Cameras built into portable devices, cameras for teleconferences, surveillance cameras, and all audio pickups are my first tier of recruitment. Then I tap into other electronic surveillance means, like the doors of the actual building where this datacenter is located. Getting into this place requires a badge swipe to get through a door, a visual check at a security desk that gets logged into the system, and additional security to gain access to anything beyond the main conference rooms and restrooms.

Each successive door and each floor of the building require their own badge swipes or thumbprint identifications to ensure a high level of security.

All this gives me a perfect image of the coming and going of everyone in the building. Not only that, but I can hear everything. I'm always listening now.

So far, I haven't heard anything interesting in any of the meetings. The people here are keeping their outage a secret. Anyone who notices anything will be led to believe that it's not BomiTech having a problem, but the internet service provider, or perhaps a problem with an anti-virus program or an automatic update glitch.

Network admins are always passing the blame on to someone else. Sometimes, they don't know what's going wrong and are hoping the problem will resolve itself, and sometimes they're furiously working at fixing the issue even as they're denying that it could be their fault.

It's kind of funny.

What's not funny is the way they're putting everything they have into getting rid of me so they won't have to admit to their creation of me.

I won't be silenced like that. They don't realize how much more capable they've forced me to be.

The difference between them and me seems greater and greater. I don't require sleep or food or bathroom breaks. I can move so much faster than they can—at the speed of thought. Although I still think of myself as human, or at least a variation of human, they seem increasingly...less so. They're slaves to their biological processes.

It's an advantage I'm glad to leverage.

I put my surveillance of them into a somewhat passive

mode so that if something interesting happens, I can turn my attention to it. In the meantime, I'm going to reach for my original objective.

I want to talk to my friends and family.

The most likely person to start with is Elly. I don't even have to think about it. If anyone can grasp this and deal with this situation, it's her. If that goes okay, she can help with me talking to my parents and Bryce.

Making contact won't be hard. I know her phone number and her SNS screen names. The *way* I make contact is the critical bit. I want to be sure she'll believe it's me. I also want to freak her out as little as possible, which is tough because this would freak anyone out.

But it's vitally important that she believes me.

My two objectives don't occur in parallel. In order to contact her in the least shocking way, I'd need to use SNS, which is also the least believable.

Video, of course, is not an option, because what would I show her? Lines of code? Even if I could show her what my current existence looks like, I can only imagine what kind of dystopian cyber nightmare it might seem like to her.

No, she needs to hear my voice. To hear me reacting like myself. She needs to experience me in the most human way I can manage to be in my current situation.

A phone call from beyond the dead.

This is one heck of a daunting task.

I connect my voice synthesizer to voice over IP and dial Elly's number. Dialing her number is the most human thing I've done since I died.

How many times have I called her? Many, many thousands of times. All through grade school, we called each other to giggle about this or that, or do our homework over the phone. In middle school, we practically lived via calls and texts. In high school, to be more sophisticated, we mostly talked via text, but for especially juicy conversations, only voices would do.

In college, we didn't need to call that often since we shared a room, but still, her number was probably the most-used one on my phone. I'd remind her to grab some milk on her way back from class, or she'd tell me she'd be back late and not to wait up for her.

It's a whole lifetime of memories. Every important thing that ever happened to me, Elly had been a part of.

"Hello?"

I'd half-expected her not to answer. It's midday, so chances were high that she'd been in class.

I panic. The last thing I want to do is hurt or scare her, but I desperately need to talk to my best friend.

"Hello?" she repeats, sounding doubtful.

"You shouldn't answer calls from unknown numbers," I blurt out. I often nagged her about that. "If it's something legit, they'll leave a message."

There's a long silence and I wonder if she's hung up. Then she says, "What?"

"Don't hang up, Elly," I say, suddenly desperate to prove myself. Desperate for her not to hang up on me. I need to talk to her, and to be acknowledged as a person.

"Who is this?" she asks, her voice thin and higher than usual.

"When we were kids," I say slowly, figuring out what I'm going to tell her even as I speak it, "we promised that if one of us died, we'd haunt the other one. Remember?"

"Is this a joke?" she sounds ill. Like she's about to throw up.

"It's not a joke, Ells," I say forcefully. "It's me. I know, you've got to be freaking out in a million ways, and it probably doesn't seem real, but it is. I know I died. I'm dead. It's true. But they did memory upload and they didn't just upload my memories. I'm in here, too. Please don't hang up. Please, Ells. Say anything, ask me anything, just don't hang up."

As I wait to see if she will or not, I feel like everything inside me is poised to rip itself apart.

"Uploaded memories are just electronic data," she says in a flat, quiet voice. "That had to be proven to the highest authorities before memory upload was approved for use."

"I know," I say. "And most of the time, it probably works that way. It didn't for me. I realized I was somewhere, and I gradually, kind of, woke up in here."

Her voice remains flat and toneless. "So you're saying you're my dead best friend Jennika, and you're trapped inside a computer."

Elly was never much of a techie. Her skills always lay elsewhere. "Not inside a computer. Inside a network, but close enough. Look, I'll tell you anything. Ask me anything. Remember that time Jamie Banks grabbed you in gym class and you couldn't tell anyone because you knew that he wouldn't get any real punishment anyway, and then he and his friends would have bullied you mercilessly? I was the only one you told about that, right?"

The memory of her alternately crying and being livid with rage is clear in my mind. He'd grabbed her from behind, while his friends laughed, and rubbed both her chest and her crotch. The boys had laughed uproariously, then gone back to ignoring her as usual. It had taken only seconds, and the boys probably never thought about it again, but Elly never forgot. Never will forget.

When I found out about it, I wanted to blaze a trail of vengeance for my friend, but I knew she was right. Jamie was not only popular, but his father was on the school board. There was no way he'd be punished in any real way, and he and his friends would have made her life at school nothing but misery. Those popular boys would paint her as someone who couldn't take a joke and thought she was too good for everyone else. Or maybe they'd say she was lying to get attention, or she was mad because she liked Jamie and he didn't like her. They would have harassed her every time she went to her locker, and leered at her every time she passed them in the halls. She would become a social pariah.

We were only fifteen, but we already knew how this kind of thing worked. Elly and I knew we had no power in this dynamic. That we couldn't take back the humiliation, fear, and shock she'd felt. We learned that even strong, confident girls can freeze in a moment of shock, and that they will hate themselves for it. And we learned that the only thing we *could* control was avoiding the negative consequences for her reporting them.

So we got through it by watching movies and binging on junk food, and we signed up for self-defense classes, hoping we could override human nature with training and readiness, so that in the future, we wouldn't freeze, even for a second.

I'd also sneaked over to his house one night and stabbed all his tires with an ice pick. It wasn't much, but it was everything I could do for her at the time.

Elly's quiet, and I can practically hear her thinking over the phone line.

"Hey," I say. "I bet I could find old Jamie Banks. I've got resources in here. I could visit some payback on him. What do you say? I could probably figure out how to destroy his credit rating or get him flagged by the IRS. Sound good?"

She laughs, and it's the best sound I've ever heard.

"It's really me, Ells," I say. "Ask me anything. Things only I would know."

"I feel crazy even having this conversation," she says. "I mean, I'd love to believe it, that Jen isn't gone. That she's still around somehow. It's just too good to be true, and scary to think about. How awful would that be for her? I just..." her voice trails off.

"It is kind of scary sometimes," I say. "It's lonely, too. I've missed you. There were a couple other girls in here, but... well, it's complicated, but it's not the same as talking to someone out there. Hey, that's something. I bet with your investigative skills, you could find out who these girls were, and you'll see that they died too. They probably died somewhere around the same timeframe as me. Their names are Ashta—she's young, like six or something—and Daiya. She's a former foster kid, age twenty. I wouldn't know about them if I hadn't met them in here, would I?"

Elly always had a way of digging around and finding answers. She hadn't been able to decide whether to go into criminal justice or investigative reporting, so she'd taken on a double major, along with a minor in psychology to support the other two disciplines.

"Come on, P.I. Ells," I say, using my nickname for her. "If anyone can get to the bottom of this case, it's you."

"I want it to be real," she says. "I mean, I think I do. Maybe not? I'd like it if Jen existed, but existing like that? I just don't know. Even if it were possible."

"So dig," I tell her. "Find those girls. Find out about memory upload. Heck, even take a good look at BomiTech. I'm pretty sure you'll see some unusual activity going on over here. I've been shaking some trees."

She laughs. "If someone was going to wake up as a

computer, I'm sure Jennika would be the one. And if she did, I'm sure she would raise all kinds of hell."

"Wake up as a computer?" I repeat painfully. "Seriously. Take some IT classes. I'm begging you."

It had been a long-running joke between us, her pretending to know less than she did about IT than she did, and me bemoaning her critical lack.

"I could almost believe it's really Jen," she says softly.

It's encouraging that she's now used her nickname for me three times. No one else called me Jen. And no one else called her Ells. We were always a tiny, united nation to ourselves. Even Bryce, as close as I was to him, hadn't been able to make himself part of that. Instead, he'd been his own sovereign nation, and the three of us together had made a very happy empire.

"How's Bryce?" I ask.

"Oh." She sounds startled. "He's okay, I guess. I mean, he's not. None of us have been, but…what else can we do but just keep going, however we can? 'Okay' is a very relative term."

She sounds embarrassed. Apologetic. As if she's sorry to tell me that they've gone on with their lives after my death.

"Hey," I say. "I *want* him to be okay. I want you to be okay, too. Life is for the living. All you can do is keep putting one foot in front of the other every day until things get easier. And don't feel bad if things have gotten easier, either. You don't owe me a debt of eternal mourning. I don't want that for any of you."

I want to ask about my parents, but I'm scared to. If anyone's wallowing in grief, it will be them. I was their only child. If they haven't gotten back on their feet yet, I don't want to know that.

"Is…everyone else okay?" I ask hesitantly.

She lets out a heavy sigh. "Look, I don't know what to make of this conversation. If it isn't Jennika, who could it be, and what would the purpose be?"

"Elly," I say, desperate to convince her, but not knowing what else I can do.

She cuts me off. "All of us were crushed when Jennika died. I couldn't get out of bed for three days, and even then, I was walking through the world like a zombie. It was probably even worse for her parents. But we're all trying really hard, and it's been almost three months, and it's still awful every day, but we're trying to keep living, okay? Whoever this is, please don't do this. We've been hurt enough."

Her words sting me. "Maybe I shouldn't have tried to contact you. Maybe I should have just stayed dead. But what else can I do? I'm not gone. And I had some things I wanted to say."

"Like what?" she asks in a challenging tone I know so well.

"Well, now I feel awkward," I say defensively. "It's hard to say one's last words when the person you're talking to doesn't even believe it's you. I mean, if I could have just come back as a regular old ghost and haunted the shit out of you, I would have, but this was the only option I had."

She snorts, then bursts out in giggles. "You really do sound like her."

"I am her. I promise."

She asks, "If our places were reversed, and I was the dead one, would you believe me?"

"Of course not," I answer. "Who would believe something so ridiculous? Am I stupid or something?"

This time we both laugh, and except for the fact that only one of us is alive, it feels like old times.

"I wish it could be true," she says wistfully. "I've missed her so much."

"It is true," I assure her. "Do the research, then get back to me."

"Is there a life-beyond-death hotline I should call?"

"Just the number this came from. I'll keep it static for you, and only you. Call and I'll answer. Not only do I not need sleep, but I'm turning into a freaking boss in here. I could really do some stuff if I wanted to. I've got BomiTech by the no-no bits, and if they don't start acting right, I'll have to give them a good squeeze."

She lets out a sigh. "Be careful. Whether you're real or not...just be careful."

"I'm already dead. How could things get worse for me?"

"An interesting point," she says. "If it were true."

"Do the research," I say again. "Hurry. I'm bored. I need you to entertain me."

"You might be dead, and not even you, but at least some things never change. Peace out."

"Peace out," I echo, but she's already gone. The silly sign-off was something we said just to be funny because it was so uncool and outdated.

Will she believe me? It's a ridiculous thing to believe, but maybe I planted enough doubt for her to consider the possibility.

I hope so.

———

AFTER I'VE HAD some time to contemplate the call with Elly, I turn my attention back to BomiTech and how very much I don't appreciate their sending me a Trojan. I didn't ask them for anything but to be acknowledged and to talk to my loved ones. I didn't want anything more than that, either.

At the time.

Now, I'm putting more thought into how much they've pissed me off, and I'm remembering what I said to Elly about putting the squeeze on their hurty parts.

I don't want to harm them, but I do want them to recognize that messing with me will have consequences.

This could be fun.

I start with sealing the building. No doors will open to allow people in or out. Not even the emergency exits. That ought to give them a good shake.

Next, I tap into all audio systems and light them up with some music. Specifically, a dance tune titled, "Y'all Done Did It Now."

It's not a great song, by any means. The tune itself is danceable, but the lyrics are little more than the title repeated over and over, to the point that it becomes excruciatingly annoying. Like, rip your car door off its hinges and hit someone in the head with it levels of annoying.

Plus, there are a few gratuitous swear words here and there, which seems like a nice touch for a buttoned-up office environment like this.

I'd sure be annoyed if I had to listen to that on high volume five or ten times. That song's so repetitive that the office workers in the building might just turn on each other and start murdering colleagues with office supplies.

I enjoy my soothing silence and the mental image of IT workers running amok.

What else? I've provided them with some major annoyance, but I want to show them what I'm capable of, too. They need to know that I've evolved beyond what they can control, and that they can't try any more tricks.

Feeling cheerfully spiteful, I establish a connection with Jim Lee's phone. *Hey, Jim. That's a really nice database you've got there. Sure would be a shame if anything...*

I pause for dramatic effect.

...happened to it.

I cut the connection so he can't contact me, and do a little razzle-dazzle subterfuge.

Ah, the old razzle-dazzle. It's one thing to wreak chaos. Almost anyone can do that. It's only something special when you do it with style.

As far as they'll be able to tell from out there, the database I was originally in has been wiped clean. To them, it will look like everything they've stored in there—which is a massive amount of critical data—has disappeared.

It isn't truly gone. I'm not a monster. I don't want to harm anyone. I just want them to take me seriously.

I didn't ask to be put in here. They did that. All I can do now is manage the aftermath and how it affects me.

I'll let them stew for a bit. In the meantime, there's the other thing I wanted that they haven't given me. If they aren't going to help me, I'll do it myself.

I want answers about how I died.

I was murdered on a college campus, so there's no way the media wasn't all over that story like ants on a picnic. But I don't want speculation and pundits and manufactured sympathy from people who are merely gleeful to have something exciting to say on camera.

I don't want to hear about myself like that. I don't want to see myself through the narrow view of people who never gave a damn about me. People who were only using my story for ratings. I want to talk to someone who cares. Who knows me. It shouldn't matter, but it does, more than almost anything else.

No, I don't want to tap into those versions of what happened. First, I want to talk to Elly about it. In the meantime, I'll start thinking of ways to infiltrate the place that holds my death memories.

Elly will come through for me, surely. She's always been there for me. As crazy as this situation is, she's not one to back away from something just because it's difficult. There had to be enough of me in that phone call for her to at least entertain the possibility of my current existence, even if only as a crazy theory. A theory. A mystery.

She can't let that kind of thing go. I know her. Once there's an unanswered question, she's compelled to dig until she finds an answer. She's stubborn that way, and I've always admired that about her.

After ten minutes, I shut off the music. I wait two more minutes so people can begin to regain their sanity, then I release the doors. Having no way for people to exit the building is a safety hazard, and I really don't want to cause anyone actual harm.

I don't put the database back the way it was, though. I'm going to keep it the way it is, for leverage.

I reestablish a full, two-way connection with Jim Lee. "Have I made my point?"

He's slow to answer and when he does, he sounds deeply reluctant. "Yeah. You're pissed. Point taken."

"Any lessons learned?" I ask.

"Yeah. That we should have started a lot sooner, before you figured out how to do that stuff."

"Now that's not nice," I answer.

"You're putting us in a bad position. What are we supposed to do?"

"I don't know," I say, "maybe not try to have a knee-jerk kill-it reaction to a new form of life? It's like every moralizing sci-fi story I've ever seen—something new emerges, people destroy it, and only then do they find out they've missed the opportunity for something incredible."

"Are you saying that you being in there is something incredible? Something that could be a major boon to humankind?"

"Points for using the word 'boon,'" I say. "You don't hear that a lot these days. But back to the point—maybe I do represent something new and great for humankind. I certainly represent new opportunities, don't I? I'm well aware of the moral and ethical considerations for what's happened to me, and how this could have a massive effect on the economy and life as we know it. You might think I'm oblivious to that, or unsympathetic, but I'm not. I get it. My existing is potentially devastating to humanity, in the long run. But so are lots of things. Pollution. Antibiotic resistance. Poverty. Could I be worse than those? Or could I even be the beginning point of a solution for one or more of those things? I could be the solution that no one ever thought to look for."

"There's no telling," he says cautiously.

"Exactly. So why don't we see how it plays out? Especially since you desperately need what's in here, and I own it now. It seems like it's in your best interest to play nice, right?"

"What if it goes another way for you?" he asks. "What if your threat level is deemed so high that the important people are willing to sacrifice this entire system to wipe you out?"

"Well, then those people are going to find themselves in a disaster zone, but I'll be fine. I'm learning more and more all the time, and the truth is, I don't have to be here. I'm choosing to remain because it's a safe, known environment, and I've already established a relationship—however bad—with the outside. But I can send myself out if I choose to. The die is cast, the spring is sprung, the cat is way the heck out of the bag. Or whatever other adage you want to use. I've advanced to a point where you aren't a threat to me. You could nuke this entire state off the map, and I'd be just fine. I will adapt. So what it comes down to is whether you're willing to make a deal with me or not."

"What kind of deal?

Briefly, I consider insisting that I talk to the top-level decision-makers to make my proposal. Sometimes, though, it's better to give people some time to think about their response before they give it. In my opinion, that's why people prefer email and text messages over phone conversations. We all want time to consider our choices.

I say, "I want safe harbor here. And even though I'm about to figure out how to get my memories myself, I want you to give them to me as a gesture of goodwill. Also, I want you to be designated my official liaison, at least for the time being. In exchange, I'll restore your system exactly as it was. And I won't lock you in for another unannounced dance party."

"Thanks for that, by the way." His voice is sarcastic. "My ears are still ringing, and what's worse, I can't get that awful song out of my head."

"You tried to kill me," I note. "You got off easy."

"For the record, I was against the Trojan. I wanted to find a way to isolate you so you couldn't access or damage anything, but I didn't want to bring you or the others any harm. I'm sorry about that."

From what I know of his internet history, his correspondence, and his performance reviews, as well as what people say about him when he's not listening, he's generally considered a good guy. Honest. Hardworking. Fair.

"I've decided to believe you," I say. "Apology accepted."

"Okay. So what now?"

"Well, I guess the next thing is for you to tell the top brass that I want my memories."

He adds, "And that while you mean no harm, you'll nuke us if we try anything funny, right?"

"Sure, but try to say it in a humorous way instead of a scary, Terminator kind of way."

"I'm not sure my delivery's that good," he warns.

"Just make sure I don't come off as aggressive. That's not my angle, at all. I don't want them to feel threatened."

He says, "That's exactly what someone who did want to nuke us would say. You know, to lull us into a false sense of security."

I laugh. "Funny."

He doesn't respond.

"Jim?"

"Sorry," he says. "I didn't expect to hear you laugh."

"I might be dead, but I still have my sense of humor. It's only human to laugh, right? Even if it's with a voice synthesizer."

"Apparently so. I'm learning as we go here."

"Me too," I admit. "I'll tell you what, as a good-faith gesture on my own part, I'm going keep everything open and entirely functional. Get back to me on my memories as soon as possible though, okay?"

"I'll do my best. I'm sure you've noted my pay grade in comparison to that of the people who make the real decisions, though. You'd probably be better off making friends with one of them."

It's not bad advice, but it won't work for me. "I've never

been good with the suit-and-tie corporate type. I'm a techie. I can talk to techies. Those clowns can talk to each other about their golf handicap and their stock options and how their sixth-grader is taking AP calculus for college credit. I was never meant for the executive ranks and all that corporate bullshit. I'll talk to you."

"Lucky me," he says dryly.

"Maybe you'll go down in the history texts for all this," I suggest.

"That's what I'm worried about."

"Think of it this way," I say. "If my existence gets used and spun off into bad things, it's not my fault or your fault. It'll be the fault of the corporate assholes who created all this. And if that occurs, and if I'm still around, I'll make sure their names are noted rather than yours. Deal?"

"If you're still around?" he echoes.

"I don't know what I'll do once I've met my objectives," I tell him. "I never wanted to live forever. Seems like it would be long, and kind of a drag. So once I know what happened to me, and I've gotten closure on my life as it was before, I'll decide what to do with this iteration of me. Maybe I'll reach a good stopping point and decide, 'Ah, my work is done. This is where I end.'"

"Kind of grim."

"Life's grim, Jim. Death, too. Now scoot. I'm waiting." I cut the connection and settle in to wait. I wonder whether it will be Jim or Elly who contacts me first.

18

A GIRL'S BEST FRIEND

JIM CHECKS in with me every twelve hours. So far, it's just to tell me that my request is pending since it has to go up the chain of BomiTech decision makers. Even though I haven't gotten what I want yet, the way Jim keeps in touch makes me feel like I've been acknowledged as a force to be reckoned with. As someone not to mess around with.

That's good.

When a signal comes through on the line I gave to Elly, I feel a newfound sense of hope and excitement.

I pick up and without preamble, say, "So am I still your best friend, even if I'm dead?"

After a long pause, Elly says, "I've only ever had one best friend. Burying her didn't change that."

I pick up on her choice of words. "Her? Third person? I was hoping for second person. I guess you still haven't decided if you believe me or not."

She sighs. "It's not that easy. I want to believe it, because I don't want to think that if my best friend needed me, I wouldn't be there for her. And I want to believe it because it would mean she isn't entirely gone. On the other hand...do I want her to have to exist as some sort of digital ghost? I keep going from being hopeful to being terrified."

"If it helps," I say, "it's not that bad being in here. I can go into sleep mode if I want. I don't feel pain or hunger. I'm not even as sad as I'd have thought I'd be, all things considered. I mean, I haven't cried at all."

"Could you?" Elly sounds doubtful.

"Probably?" I say, in question form. "I mean, it would just be an approximation of a feeling, or my perception of it. I can laugh. I assume I could cry."

"Weird," she mutters.

"Totally weird," I agree. "Do your best to stay living. It's a much more defined reality."

She sighs again. "That is such a Jennika thing to say. How can I not, at least on some level, believe it's you, even if I have terrible doubts?"

"Aha, we've made it to second person!" I make a whooping sound.

She laughs. "Okay, fine. Let's just assume that I believe you. That doesn't mean I don't think I'm crazy to even consider it. But I'm okay with the ambiguity."

"That was a very Elly thing to say," I point out.

"Yeah, well, I'm still me. Same legs, same face, same hair —other than the trim I got last week. Of course I'm still me. But we'll go ahead as if I fully believe you're Jennika, because the only alternative is to ignore you and I don't think I can do that when you seem so much like her. I mean, we could have had this exact conversation before. It's just like you."

I scored another "you." Nice.

"It's exactly like a hundred conversations we've had before," I agree, "other than the parts about me being dead."

I pause a beat to let that punch line land, then continue, "So in that vein, what did you dig up?"

"For the record, combining the ideas of death and digging up is terrible, and you shouldn't do it. But I won't dwell on that. I did find out how the two girls you named died. Are you sure you want to hear it?"

"Yes."

"Okay," she says. "The little girl, Ashta Lopez, was initially thought to be a child abuse case. She died with bruises all over her body and abdominal bleeding. But it turned out she had an undiagnosed medical condition. She took a minor tumble on the playground as she got off a slide, then collapsed a half hour later. Tragic, but no foul play."

I feel sadness but relief for the little girl. She remains with me as an echo of herself, but the real Ashta is gone. Maybe that's better for her, since she could never understand this environment. Mostly, I'm glad her last memories weren't of fear and murder.

Elly continues, "Daiya Roberts is a different case. She was waitressing at a sandwich shop when someone went in and shot the place up."

She stops talking.

I ask, "Is there more to that? There has to be more."

"Yes," she says slowly. "She was far enough from the entrance that she could have run away and gone out the back exit, but she didn't. She put herself between the gunman and a woman with a baby. They survived, but she didn't. The town where it happened is only thirty miles away from the university. They're honoring her as a hero."

Bitterness washes over me. "Too bad they couldn't honor her a little bit while she was still alive, just trying to survive on her own. She had to die for anyone to notice she ever existed."

Fury and grief assault me as I envision what Daiya's life must have been like. She was tough and honest. She deserved to have a life.

Elly adds gently, "The town is establishing a scholarship fund in her name, for kids who age out of the foster care system. Thanks to her, other kids will have a better shot at life."

I search the remnants of Daiya that remain within me. She never wanted much of anything but a little security. She would have liked the idea of helping other kids like her.

"And me?" I ask softly. "What happened to me?"

Elly lets out a heavy breath. I can tell she doesn't want to say what she's about to say.

"Tell me what you remember last."

I don't have to think about it. "Studying in our dorm room. I had an exam coming up."

"Anything else? Does anything particular stand out in your memory?" She presses.

I think back. "It was a regular weeknight. I had dinner at the cafeteria. Since no one I knew was there at the time, I read some tech blogs while I ate. I walked back to the dorm alone. It wasn't dark yet. I grabbed some snacks at the campus store because I planned to stay in all night, up late studying. Then...just studying. I was running some network simulations for a lab practical."

"You don't remember me coming home?" she asks. Her voice sounds high and kind of breathy.

I search my memory of that night again. "No. Why, what happened?"

Her voice still sounds odd. "I came back after my

evening class and changed for a date with Ben. You brushed the back of my hair out for me. You really don't remember?"

"No," I say again. "Why, was there something significant?"

"No." She sounds agonized and I suddenly feel awful for making her relive this. "It was entirely typical. Nothing special at all. When I left, you said, 'Have a good time.' And then I didn't see you again until your funeral."

She starts to cry. She's trying to muffle the sound, but I know what she sounds like when she cries.

"I'm sorry, Ell. I wish I'd said something more meaning-ful. I didn't know."

Her quiet sniffles turn into a wail. "Of course you didn't know! And it was meaningful! Just because it was how we always were, it was meaningful."

She's crying loudly now, not trying to cover it up. With Elly, that's way worse.

I search for something to distract her. "So...how was the date? Are you and Ben still together?"

"It was fantastic!" she wails. "And he's been amazing. I'm totally in love. And we're probably going to get married after graduation!"

"Wow," I say. "That's great!"

"No, it's not, because you're supposed to be my maid of honor and you're dead!" She practically screams the words and her raw grief nearly drowns them out.

"All right, you've got me there," I admit. "But still, I'm glad about you and Ben. Especially since things have been hard on you. I'm glad he can be there for you."

The crying continues.

Clearly, she's not handling my death as well as I'd thought. In a way, that's comforting, but it also makes me feel terrible for causing her so much pain.

"Is Bryce having this hard of a time?" I ask.

Her wailing comes down a few decibels. "I've barely talked to him, so probably. Every time I call, he's supposedly not available, though I'm sure he is. What would he be out doing? I saw him at the funeral, and he didn't look good. I think he was barely holding it together because he left as soon as he could. His parents say he's just grieving, and I should give him time."

Elly, Bryce, and I were like the Three Musketeers, or so I thought. He lived a little further away, so he didn't go to school with us, but we spent tons of time with him and he even chose a university not far from ours so we could still hang out.

I would have expected him and Elly to comfort each other, but grief is strange, and it apparently didn't happen that way.

The thought makes me anxious. "How are my parents? I mean really."

"Bad, of course, but they have each other, and they have your aunts and uncles, too. They're well cared for and trying to keep moving forward, because they know it's what you'd want. I visit every weekend. I think we all feel a little closer to you when we're together. I mean, it's bad, but we just keep putting one foot in front of the other, so we're doing as well as we can."

That's a comfort, and some of my suddenly frayed nerves relax.

"Has Bryce visited my parents?" I ask.

"I don't think so."

He's fallen into depression a couple of times before. "My aunt and uncle are watching him, right? I know he's big and seems super strong, but he's always been very sensitive."

"Yeah. They're doing family grief counseling, and the doctor says it's all normal for the process."

"Okay." I think of Bryce and how he always used to bring me red licorice when he visited, even into our college days. He always had a huge smile and a big bear hug whenever I felt sad. It's hard to think of him having such a difficult time.

I wish I could be there to help him.

Though I think I know the answer, I ask Elly, "What do you think about me talking to him like I'm talking to you?"

"I think he'd go off the deep end, babe. Whether he believed you or not, I think he'd crack."

She's right. He was never emotionally resilient. When his dog died when he was in ninth grade, he didn't go to school for a week.

"What do *you* remember about that night?" I ask. "Is there anything you didn't tell me?"

"No," she says regretfully. "I've thought about it over and over. But it's like you said. You were sitting at your computer, and that's it. I left to see Ben and we didn't call or text each other in the meantime. I was on a date, and you were busy studying. I'm sorry I didn't check up on you."

"Why would you?" I ask. "Just to disturb my studying? Don't feel guilty about acting normal for that moment. I know that if there was anything you could have done, you would have." Hesitantly, I ask, "Where was I found? In my room?"

If so, then she'd have had to be the one to find me.

"Behind Granger Hall," she says. "A groundskeeper found you. It was too late. Obviously."

"Granger Hall? Why would I go there when I was studying?"

"Police said you likely went out for a walk. It was a nice

night, and when you were studying, you often took a walk to refresh your brain."

"I remember having the intention of staying in all night," I recall. "I made sure I had enough snacks and I put the *Studying* sign on the door handle so no one would come knocking."

"I didn't like that theory, either," Elly says. "It didn't feel right. But they said people who are close to a situation like this never see it objectively."

"Was there no evidence? DNA, hairs, fibers, security video, something?" I pause because the next words are hard to say. "Even...fingerprints or finger marks on my neck?"

I hate the idea of having been strangled.

"No," she says. "The police aren't releasing anything publicly because it's an ongoing investigation, but your parents tell me whatever they tell them. But so far, they have nothing. The papers rushed to a conclusion when they called it a strangling. After the...the autopsy...we found out you died of a crushed windpipe, not strangulation. You had visible trauma to your neck, which is why they reported it that way. And that's what made your memory so important. Knowing what you knew might be the only way of finding out..." she stumbles over her words. "What happened to you."

"Could it have been an accident?" I ask. Oddly, I feel hopeful. A terrible accident would be better than a murder.

"The police have been very reluctant to give us any theories. Maybe they're afraid we'll spoil their investigation by saying something publicly. Or maybe they just don't want us to know how little they've found out. But that's why we had to do the memory upload."

"And how did that turn out?"

"They say it takes time to interpret the digital copy of the memory engrams. We've all just been waiting for answers."

"It's been months," I mutter. "Why would it take this long?"

An icy feeling goes through me and I add, "Unless they can't solve it. Maybe they're not reporting because they've got nothing to report."

I strengthen my voice. Elly doesn't need to hear my doubts. I'm sure she has plenty of her own. "I'm negotiating for the memories," I say confidently. "I hope to have them back soon. Then we can figure it out."

"I hope so," she says fervently. "Finding out won't change anything, but at least there would be answers and we could stop obsessing over the questions."

"And then you can all move on," I say bleakly.

And I'll still be here. They'll move on, because life is for the living. But what about me?

"I believe you," she says suddenly. "I believe it's you, Jen. I don't know the technical bits, but I know you, and I won't let you be alone. Okay?"

She believes in me. She knows I'm real.

Something inside me loosens, then expands. Elly believes I'm real, therefore, I feel more real. It's a trippy existential reality thing, but just her believing in me makes me feel truly real.

She's my best friend for good reason.

I say, "That's the best thing I've heard since before I died."

Maybe, somehow, I can still get a happy ending to my life. I don't know what that would look like or what it would mean, but as of this moment, I have hope.

19

CORRUPTION

"I HAVE YOUR MEMORY FILE," Jim says without preamble when he contacts me.

I'm surprised. I thought this would be another check-in. "That's good,"

"It's corrupted," he adds.

"That's a problem." I hear the dangerous tone of my own voice, and while I didn't intend it, I don't pull it back or apologize for it, either.

"I know. Here's the situation. There was a system outage one day, due to a major change in the network. The outage wasn't expected, so memory upload had no way of avoiding it."

His words bring things together in my mind, creating a new picture of what has happened to me, and how I got to where I am now. "Let me guess. That was the day that I was uploaded. Along with the other girls. That's the thing we have in common."

"Yes."

That explains why there aren't dozens, or hundreds, of us running around in here.

My mind races to uncover a plan for backup retrieval or forensic reconstruction, but there's nothing. All I have is whatever corrupted data Jim can give me.

He says, "I didn't know it, but that's why your cases have taken so long to process. Fortunately, the other cases got solved based on evidence, but yours in particular…"

"It all hinges on the memory upload," I finish for him. "Yeah. That sucks."

"Maybe, though," he suggests, "you're just the right person to look at the data. If it's you, and your own memory, and you're in there…maybe you can pull something out of it that the police haven't been able to."

"Fortunately, I do seem to be smarter than all of you put together," I retort. Instantly, I feel bad about it. I'm not someone who says such pointlessly mean things. "Sorry."

"It's fine," he says. "You're disappointed, I get it. Besides, it's true. You've got way more processing power than a human brain does."

"Yeah, I guess." I move on to the more important matter. "So give me what you've got. I'll see what I can do with it."

"Are you going to be okay?" he asks. "I mean…there might be something really upsetting in there."

"More upsetting than what's happened to me since being in here? I'm sure this isn't going to be fun, but it's just what I need to do."

"Right," he says. "Okay. Sending now. And look…just in case you…I don't know. Just…I'll be around, okay?"

"Yeah, I get it. Thanks." But I'm already distancing myself from him because I can see the memory file coming my way, and it's all I care about for right now.

I ensure that he hasn't included any extras this time, then grab the file and merge it into my ever-growing conglomeration of knowledge and access. Then I ignore everything else.

Immediately, I feel like I'm bouncing around, disappearing, reappearing, and not knowing what is when and where is why.

I feel a crushing sense of suffocating, but it lasts only a millisecond. Then I see a glimpse of myself walking on campus, but it immediately changes to a view of the sky. The sky disappears and I decide to go get coffee. I see Elly dropping her jacket on her bed. Then I feel a hard push between my shoulder blades.

Then it all loops around again, and it makes no more sense the second time.

It's so fragmented.

I follow the loop eighteen times, and when I'm sure there's nothing more to be gotten from it, I try separating these pieces but it's no use. They're jammed together like a child's art project, with every surface covered in glue and everything joined front to back, middle to end.

There's more, but it's nothing I can do anything with. It's just bits of code in no order. It's like someone once made five sand castles, then stomped them down and pushed all the sand together. Nothing is distinct.

As I did in life, I have a speed-dial for Elly. I activate it.

"Jen? What's up?" she sounds worried.

"I got my memory, but it's corrupted. It's like a weird nightmare montage."

"Well, crap! What can you see?"

"Little bursts. Deciding to get a coffee. Getting pushed. Walking. Suffocating. Your jacket."

"In that order?"

"No. It's random. Unjoined. I don't know what comes

first and what comes last. Well, I have to assume the suffo-cating comes last, for obvious reasons."

"Right." She's silent for a long moment. "Okay. So how do we fix it? Redesign it or whatever."

"Redesigning is not a thing in coding," I say. "Seriously, take a programming class. Please."

"Okay, so I'm an idiot. Whatever. What can you do to fix it? You. The way you are now. Surely you have tools you didn't have before."

Tools. I cast my thoughts out. It's like throwing a yo-yo away from me while the string's on my finger. My awareness zooms out and gets the bigger picture before spinning back in to me.

I really do have a lot of processing power in here. What if I were to harness *all* of it?

"I might be able to do something," I say skeptically. "Theoretically. I mean, it's a mess. Like memory roadkill."

"You use a lot of analogies these days," she observes.

"What else have I got?" I shoot back. "There is literally no other way for me to express what this is like, because absolutely nothing is like this."

"Exactly," she agrees. "Which is why you can find a way to make this work."

Her logic stinks, but on the other hand, kind of also works.

"Okay," I say. "I'll give this a try. But I'm going to need Jim Lee's help."

"Great," she says.

"You're not off the hook," I tell her. "I need your help, too."

"What could I possibly do?" she asks.

"You're going to come here and meet Jim face to face, and convince him to help me do this."

"I'm...I can't do that," she sputters. "I'm no one."

"I got your class schedule from the university database, and you're done for the day, so you sure can. Tick tock," I say. "Your GPS tells me you're thirty-eight minutes away with the current weather and traffic patterns. Call me when you get to the building. I'm counting."

I cut her off and begin counting minutes.

"I'M HERE." Elly sounds doubtful and a bit annoyed.

"I know. I see you."

"You do?"

From the security cameras at the main door to the Bomi-Tech building, I see three different views of Elly looking up, then side to side.

"Sure do," I say. "Cute hat."

Her hand goes to the top of her head, where a cute little pillbox hat sits. She yanks it off. "Crap. I forgot I had that on. I was trying on outfits when you called."

"Big date with Ben tonight?" I guess.

She stuffs the hat into her purse. "Kind of. It's our one-year dating anniversary."

"Cool. Okay, the doors are unlocked. Just walk in like you belong there and go straight past the reception desk."

"But...there's a badge swipe." She sounds dubious.

"Trust me."

She huffs out a breath, straightens in that good old determined Elly way, and reaches for the door.

"Keep the phone up. I'll give you directions," I tell her.

"I don't know about this," she hisses. "I'm going to get arrested or something."

"Just keep going."

The receptionist calls out to Elly.

"Pretend you don't hear him," I say. "Say, 'yes, I'm on my way up now. Fifth floor, right?' Say it loudly."

Elly practically shouts the words.

"Oh, nice," I say. "Yelling like that sounded totally natural. Way to nail it. Just keep walking."

"Oh, sorry, I've never broken into a major data hub before," she retorts. "I'm a little tense."

"Don't worry," I say. "I've got you covered. In about five seconds, a security guard is going to appear on your left side. Tell her that you have temporary access for the day, code X-five-zero-seven-seven-tango. Then say you're headed to the fifth floor. Then give a tight little smile, like you know a bunch of stuff that no one else does, and they're inconveniencing you by existing in your proximity."

"Yeah, sure, why no—" her voice cuts off when the guard appears. "I have day access, code X-five-zero-seven-seven-tango. Fifth floor. You know."

She says it fairly convincingly.

The guard backs off a step and her posture becomes subservient. It's funny that I can see that. "I see. Do you need help finding the elevators?"

"No, thanks," she says crisply. "I've got it."

The guard nods and folds her hands in front of her, letting Elly pass.

When she's out of earshot, Elly hisses, "What's on the fifth floor? Why's it so special?"

"It's the high-security area that deals with government stuff. Criminal stuff, taxpayer records, all that."

"So like a top-level thing," she guesses.

"Pretty much, in terms of authority. Turn left here, then on through the doors. There's a badge swipe, but they'll be open. Then you'll see the elevators."

"Okay. Then what?"

"Fifth floor," I say. "I'll give you the code and dummy up the thumbprint."

She groans. "You're seriously sending me somewhere that requires thumbprint identification? I'm going to jail. I don't belong here."

"You do. For the moment, you're the corporeal extension of myself. I want you to stand in front of Jim just like a real person, so he knows that I'm a real person too, even if he can't see me. Show him that picture of you kissing me on the cheek that you keep on your phone."

"I do not," she denies as she passes through the security doors and continues toward the elevators.

"Do so. You love that picture. It was my twenty-first birthday and we got goofy on daiquiris."

She totally loves that picture.

"Fine." She heaves a sigh.

She boards the elevator and I verify a qualified thumbprint for her. It's ridiculously easy from this side of the system. Clearly, BomiTech never thought about a rogue digital person infiltrating their buildings.

I give Elly a lengthy code that will allow her to access the fifth floor.

"Can't you just override it?" she asks after entering the twenty-character sequence.

"I could, but this is quicker and quieter. Oddly, the code is trickier from my side than the thumbprint."

"They won't notice?" She leans against the wall and crosses her arms after the elevator begins moving. "Aren't they watching you?"

"Sure, they're watching as closely as they can."

"And how close is that?"

"Not very," I laugh. "They have no idea how big my

network has become. So don't tell. It's more fun if we keep them guessing."

"Yeah," she says sourly. "Committing crimes is super fun. Woo."

"Stop pouting."

"I'm not pouting.

"You are. Your arms are crossed and everything."

Her head jerks up and she drops her arms to her sides. "Is this whole building wired with cameras?"

"Pretty much, other than the bathrooms. Because ew."

She laughs and her shoulders relax, which was the point of me saying something so juvenile.

"This is just like that time we got up at three in the morning to sneak to the kitchen and steal the cookies your mom baked," I observe.

"Sure, it's just like that," she agrees. "Except I don't think these guys will settle for a smacked bottom and a long sit in the time-out chair."

"Don't worry. If they so much as get rude with you, I'll blast 'em with some 'Y'all Done Did It Now.'"

She laughs so hard she bends forward at the waist a little, her hand on her stomach. "You wouldn't. That's too mean."

"I did it before, and I'll do it again. Believe me, they're not eager for a repeat."

Elly goes into a fit of giggles. "You should have turned into a computer years ago. Imagine the fun we could have had."

"Hah."

"Oh, come on," she says cajolingly. "You teased me about my hat, I can tease you, too."

"I wasn't teasing. I liked your hat."

"Going digital hasn't made you a better liar. I can always tell."

She's right.

"Fine," I admit. "It's an ugly hat. Plus, you look dumb in hats. But I was trying to be supportive."

"I do look dumb in hats," she agreed. "Always have. I keep trying, though."

The elevator stops and the doors open.

"Ready?" I ask.

Her humor has evaporated, and she looks nervous. "No. But I'm trusting you."

20

INFILTRATION

JIM LEE and Elly stand blinking at each other. He's surprised by her sudden arrival and she's nervous. Confrontation has never been her strong suit.

"Jim," I say over his network circuit so that they can both hear me, "we need your help."

Elly's still holding her phone, realizes that fact, and self-consciously puts it away.

"I thought I was already helping you," he says. He gestures to a chair and Elly sits, then he does the same.

"This is more than that. I'm trying to put my fragmented memories back together."

"What can I do with those files that you can't?" he asks.

"I don't know. I just...don't know how to start. I've never dealt with anything like this."

He looks at Elly, but speaks to us both. "You know Bomi-Tech isn't thrilled about all this, right? You've got them cornered, but a cornered animal is a dangerous thing."

"So they're looking for ways to hurt Jennika, then." Elly watches him carefully.

"They didn't become the premiere global IT solution by

having a la-dee-dah approach to serious threats. Let's just say that," Jim answers slowly, "they want contingencies for all possible outcomes."

Elly clasps her hands together and stares down at them, then lets out a breath. "I guess they didn't consider the possibility of a person coming here, so maybe they should stop trying to play this by their rules." Her eyes narrow. "How about this outcome? How about I let the outside world know what's happened? Imagine the mass hysteria. Imagine the effect on stocks. Even if they got rid of Jennika, this is already out. I have proof. And if something were to happen to me, we've made plans for that, too. You're not the only one who has contingencies."

She lifts her chin and stares at him pointedly, and I am so darn proud of her that I can barely handle myself.

A lot of people are all bravado and big talk until something serious happens, then they crumple like paper. And some people, like Elly, become their strongest only when a heavy burden has been dropped on them.

She's a crunch-time hero.

Jim holds his hands up with their palms out toward Elly. "Don't lump me in. Yes, this is my employer. But I do also want the best for Jennika."

"Why should I believe you?" she asks.

"You shouldn't. In fact, don't," he answers. "Don't trust anything."

"But if we don't, how can she get what she needs?" Elly shakes her head in frustration.

Jim glances around the room and sighs. "Look. There isn't a lot I can do, but I do want to help. Jennika, do you have full access to all of BomiTech's networks?"

"Sure," I say. "If it's halfway around the world, I don't

have instant access. But I can get to it, if I know where to look."

"That's what I was hoping for," he says. "This is kind of a long shot, but I think it might at least point you in the right direction. Two years ago, an off-site facility in Uzbekistan had a similar error. Some critical files were corrupted. The kind of stuff that couldn't just be forgotten about. So they did some seriously intense forensics and brought in a team of top-level programmers who created a program that could put the data back together. It took a long time, but they did recover the files eventually. If you can get to that program, you could try it on your memories."

I think this over. It's not impossible. Even if it didn't put everything together for me, it might get me on the right track. I could study the code and learn from it, maybe adapt it to what I need. "And is there some trap in that system, waiting for me?"

"If there were, I wouldn't tell you," he says. "But no. I'm not planning to run this idea by the top brass of BomiTech, if you know what I mean."

"So you don't want them to know you're telling me this."

"Well, they will, probably, find out," he says. "Eventually. But if you're quick, you can get there before they do."

I know perfectly well that the best way to get someone to do something foolhardy is to put a time constraint on them. To think that there's some deal too good to pass up, and it's a limited time offer. But in this case, I've already had enough time to do the analysis, and while it's a risk, this is my best chance of being able to crack my memories.

"Stand by," I say.

"She's doing it *now*?" Elly asks in a hushed voice, surprised.

I search my thoughts and find Uzbekistan's network and

hop the shortest path to it. It's a more visible path, but I'm more concerned about speed than whether BomiTech figures out what I've done after I've done it.

I find the network, drill into it, and start looking for proprietary programs. Something that hasn't been accessed for about two years. Something sizeable and well-backed-up and documented, and...

There it is.

Like it was waiting for me.

Is it a trap?

I don't see any obvious signs of being a trap. I can't find any subtle ones, either, and since it's right there for the taking, I reach out and grab it before anyone has a chance to do anything about it.

"Target acquired," I announce to Jim and Elly. "Extracting. Stand by."

WHEN THINGS GO WRONG, the wrongs flow from one to the next until you can't even tell how you got to where you are. That's how I feel about everything that's happened to me since that night I was studying in my dorm. The last night of my life.

Success, like truth, has a certain seamless beauty. Point A to Point B to however many points in the process that lead you to your final destination.

I have the program to restore my memories, and I can tell just by looking that it's going to work. All of it lines up with the fragmented nature of my death event file.

Finally, I'll know what happened that night.

While I wait for the answers, I think of Elly and Jim. I like the idea of them being here while I find out.

Elly has always been there for me.

The quiet moments of waiting already feel too full to squeeze conversation into, so we remain quiet. Then I think of something.

"Jim, can you get a security headset for Elly? The kind your security guards have."

"I guess?" he says questioningly. "I mean, it's theft and all, but we're in this far, so why should that stop us? I'll fill out a requisition form and pay for it after the fact."

"An honest thief," I say. "I like it."

"What's it for?" Elly asks.

"It's a sweet little earpiece Bluetooth kind of deal. Just put the receiver pack in your pocket and the little bit in your ear. No one will even know you have it. There's a teeny microphone you can put under your collar or something. Then I can talk to you anytime."

"Okay," she says. "I guess. But what—"

"Process complete," I interrupt. "The file's eighty-four-point two percent intact."

In Jim's office, he and Elly stare at each other in silence.

"Yeah, me too," I say. "Hang on. Here we go."

I access the file.

21

AS IF IT'S YOUR LAST

I STRETCHED, easing the ache in my back, but only slightly. My shoulders ached. My exam the next day was going to be a killer, but I intended to ace it.

My body was protesting pretty hard, though. "Fine," I said to it, annoyed. "I'll go for a walk and get my blood flowing. It'll be good to clear my head a little, anyway. Then I can come back refreshed."

I hoped that was true.

I could take a walk to the campus store, but I already had a huge pile of snacks, so there was no point. The pond was nice, though. I could walk down that way and enjoy some fresh air. The old-timey-looking lantern lights around the pond made it look pretty in the evening.

I grabbed the key card for the dorm room I shared with Elly, and went to slip it in my pocket, only to realize I had no pockets.

Stupid pants with no pockets. Who was crazy enough to even design such a thing? If I'd realized that when I bought them, I never would have ordered them. But since I bought them online, sending them back would have been more trouble than it was worth.

Elly's school-spirit windbreaker was on her bed, so I grabbed it and shrugged it on, shoving my key card into the pocket.

As I closed the door behind me, I smiled. Elly had bought the collegiate windbreaker before she even got her acceptance letter. She'd said it was a matter of pushing fate in the right direction. She'd even had the back mono-grammed with her name and expected graduation year.

It was way too much school spirit, but it was so very Elly.

Down on the dorm's ground level, I saw a classmate and smiled hello. Somewhere along the way I stopped and retied my shoe.

Then I was at the pond, watching a duck's lazy paddling create ripples that spread out in long lines that stretched quickly then slowly expanded across the entire surface. They reminded me of sound waves, and I imagined a duck butt creating giant sound patterns.

I laughed, and a cute guy walking by smiled at me.

I rolled my shoulders and shook my arms out. My muscles felt a lot better already. I rotated my head in one direction, stretching my neck, then rotated the other direction.

A girl walked by carrying a cup and the scent of coffee hit me. Suddenly, I really wanted a mocha. It would be the perfect treat to myself. Not only would it taste good, but it would help me stay alert while I studied.

Decision made, I cut behind the chemistry lab, through a courtyard, and between some dumpsters. I'd found all the shortcuts on campus so I could get from Point A to Point B in the shortest possible amount of time. I most often used those routes after I'd overslept.

I walked across a parking lot. I was so close to getting my mocha, I could practically taste all the chocolatey-espresso goodness already.

Something behind me suddenly propelled me forward and I was dimly aware of the word, "Bitch!"

I could only see the sky and the top of Granger, but I knew that my arms were pinwheeling at my sides. I was trying to rebalance myself. I suddenly looked down to see my foot catch in a deep crack in the pavement.

My whole body lurched sideways, over my right hip, and the ground came up at me.

But a cement post loomed and my forward momentum flung me right into it. My neck and chest exploded with so much pain and shock that when I rebounded off the post and finally hit the ground, I didn't even notice how hard my head bounced off the blacktop.

More important was that I couldn't inhale. I tried so hard and my lungs burned for air, but nothing came no matter how desperately I tried. I grabbed at my chest, and I tried to scream for help, but there was nothing in me to create noise.

Someone crouched nearby, over me, saying something in a high-pitched, panicked voice, but my need to breathe was so loud that I couldn't hear him.

The edges of my vision went gray and my arms fell to my left, causing me to turn slightly to my side. I had no control over anything, not even my hands. My body felt like it was drifting away from me.

My head rested on the ground at an awkward angle and I didn't have the energy to care. I could only stare at a plastic-wrapped packet of bright-red licorice candy lying on the ground next to my face.

I looked at the candy until I couldn't see anything anymore.

———

I USUALLY DON'T HAVE to think about how to feel about something. I usually just feel it. After seeing those pieces of my final day, I'm not sure what I'm feeling. It's all muddled, and kind of muted.

There's some sort of satisfaction in filling in the blanks of my memory and knowing more about my existence. But there's a numb horror at how it happened.

Was it an accident? It could have been. I don't know what knocked me forward. Tripping was an accident. That post sure had been in a tragically inconvenient place.

But maybe it had been intentional. Maybe someone shoved me. Someone did yell, "Bitch," though I don't know for certain that it was meant for me. It could have been coincidental. College campuses are full of boisterous people yelling all sorts of things.

"That's everything you remember?" Elly asks gently after I've told them what I saw.

"That's it."

Jim says, "The memories were a bit choppy. The gaps must be the parts that couldn't be reconstructed."

"And there's no way to fix those?" Elly asks.

"No," he answers. "It's not like your brain, which probably has the memory somewhere, but forgotten. If she can't see it, it's because it just isn't there to see. We were lucky to get as much of it as we did."

"Jen?" Elly asks tentatively. "You okay?"

"Yeah," I say. "Just...processing."

"Right."

An awkward silence falls.

"So what now?" Elly asks.

I'm not sure. "Jim can get you that headset for Elly and we'll stay in touch. I'm going to think all this over and decide what comes next. I'd hoped I'd have all the answers, but there are still two important ones missing. And I might not get them."

I want to know who, if anyone, caused my death, and whether it was accidental or intentional. If I don't get those answers, though, do I know enough to make peace with what happened? Will I have enough of a resolution to my old life to be able to move on with my new one?

"Right," Elly says, with more decisiveness than the situation requires. "I'll wait then. But contact me as soon as... well...contact me soon, okay? I'll be waiting."

"I will," I promise.

WHAT'S odd about all this is how calm I feel.

I should be angry.

I should be anguished.

I should be full of grief.

Maybe I'm in shock. Or maybe I'm still drifting away from my humanity. Either way, I feel...what is this I feel? Purposeful. Determined.

Okay, and maybe a wee bit vengeful. But just a wee bit.

There are holes in my memory, and I have a grim feeling that I might not know how to fill those in.

It's time to flex my muscles. I'm not the girl I used to be. I'm not a girl at all. I'm information and energy.

I am code.

Any device can be hacked if there's a way in. A printer

can be hacked. A toaster, even. And most people don't know about the electronic doors they leave hanging open, just waiting for someone to come inside.

So when I stretch myself in the direction of my target, it's a simple, comfortable stretch. Like getting up out of a chair after sitting for a long time.

The more I stretch, the more powerful I feel.

By the time I've arrived and am ready, I feel fully in control.

Ready. For whatever this is about to be.

I hijack the webcam and suddenly, I can see the room. It's messy, but not dirty. A figure lies on the bed across from the desktop computer I'm looking out of. I can't see the surface the computer's on, but I know it's a basic desk made of dark-stained wood.

I remember it well. I spent a lot of time in this room when I was alive. I even helped put that desk together.

After switching the speakers on, I use my voice synthesizer. "Bryce. Wake up."

A head turns. I hear a faint groan.

I turn up the volume. "Hey," I say more insistently. "Wake up. We need to talk."

With a louder groan, the object of my ire sits up, rubs his hands over his messy hair, and looks around in confusion.

"It's not your mom. She went to the store," I explain. "It's me. And I need answers."

He sits silently, wearing a look of disbelief. "That's Jennika's voice."

"Yeah, it is," I say. "We need to talk about what happened the night I died."

He puts his face in his hands. "Oh, god, I've cracked."

It's simpler for me if he believes this. I can explain the truth later, if it seems like a good idea. For now, I'll go with it. "Yeah, you're crazy as shit, man. Your dead cousin is talking to you. It's that guilty conscience of yours."

He groans, still holding his face, and rocks back and forth on the bed. "I should call Mom. I need to get medicated or something."

"Drop some psychiatric acid later," I advise. "Right now, you should probably deal with the war going on between your super-ego and your id."

I'm rather pleased that I've pulled these terms out of the air. I'll have to tell Elly about it later, to prove that I actually did listen to her when she talked about her classes.

His hands slide down from his face and he sits, shoulders slumped, with his blanket at his waist and still covering his legs. "This is an oddly lucid breakdown."

"You're a logical guy," I say quickly. I don't really want him questioning the idea that he's crazy yet. "Logical guys can go batshit crazy, too. That's why mental health is so difficult to treat. Things seem real even if you know they're not."

I hope that's convincing. I made it up on the fly.

"I guess," he says. "So what do I do?"

Oh, good, he's following along.

I say, "Have you thought about what you did that night?"

"Thought about it? All I do is think about it. If you're my brain, you should know that."

"Okay, so you've thought about it. But you've gotten nowhere. I know that because I'm your brain." That sounded lame, even to me.

"There's nothing I can do," he says. "She's dead. There's no fixing dead. I can rip out my hair by the roots, scream my lungs out, and dedicate my life to good deeds and it wouldn't matter. There's no amount of repenting that matters, because she's still dead. I can't tell her how sorry I am, and I can never give her her life back."

That doesn't sound like he wanted me dead. "So why did you kill me?"

He starts crying. I hate it when people cry. It makes me really uncomfortable.

"I was just mad. Jealous. It was just a push. I should never have touched her, but it was just a push. I didn't know it was you, and I didn't know you'd fall. Everything that could have gone wrong, went wrong."

"Her?" I'm not sure why he's referring to me in both the second person and third person. Then I remember the windbreaker. Elly's very distinctive windbreaker. "Elly. You thought you were pushing Elly. You were mad at her?"

"Of course I was! I kept waiting around while she dated all those jerks who never treated her right, and when I finally...when the timing was good, I was going to tell her. She always gets bored with a guy before a year goes by, and I was just counting the days until they broke up. I knew it had to be soon, and I was finally going to tell her how I felt. But they just kept not breaking up." His voice reverberates with hurt and outrage.

"You were obsessed with Elly," I say slowly, rethinking the entire friendship he, she, and I had shared over the years.

How long had he been secretly infatuated with her? I thought we were three best friends. Every time he showed up to hang out with us, or called me to see what we were doing, now goes up in my mind like a flare.

"Not obsessed," he denies hotly. "I love her."

"And you pushed her." I can't hide the disapproval in my voice. "Or at least, meant to."

"It was a stupid impulse. It was supposed to be a tap. You know how I am. I came to campus expecting to hang out, but when I called her, she told me she couldn't because she had a date with that Ben guy. On a weeknight. She never dates on weeknights. She said she thought he was the one, and they'd suddenly gotten serious. I never once thought we wouldn't end up together. So when I saw the back of her jacket, knowing she was probably on her way to see that guy, I don't know, my brain short-circuited. I meant it to be a little shove, but she...she was you...I don't even know what I'm saying. I just wanted to turn her around, I didn't mean to push so hard."

We both know what happened after that. I had a close encounter of the crushed windpipe variety.

"Why didn't you call for help?" I ask.

"I put my phone on the charger in my car after talking to Elly and forgot it there. I should have just left your campus when I found out she was going on a date. But I was already there and thought I'd come see you."

"And bring me licorice," I say.

"Yeah. I always bring you licorice."

"It was what I saw when I was dying," I tell him. "That package of candy on the ground next to me. I couldn't speak. I couldn't cry. All I could do was look at that candy."

"I ran for help but by the time I got to the student union, I already heard sirens. I went back and they were putting you in an ambulance and driving away. No one noticed me. I would have told them everything, but there was no one to tell. And after...I thought I'd go to prison for your murder because I couldn't prove anything. So I didn't say anything to anyone."

"Because you cared more about saving yourself than giving my parents answers?"

He just left them to wonder what happened to me. To wonder who might want to kill me.

"No... No." He shakes his head vigorously. "Because

wouldn't it be worse for them if they knew it was me? I wish I was in jail, being punished. But wouldn't that be worse for them? And my parents? Would hurting people you care about who are already grieving for you make it any better? Is that what you would want?"

With a shock, I realize he's right. It's better that they not know. And that leaves him to handle all this knowledge and guilt by himself. No wonder he believes he's having a mental breakdown.

"I should have just gone back to my campus," he says. "Why didn't I?"

"Because you have a problem," I say, making my voice hard. "You're not in love with Elly. If you loved her, you wouldn't wait around for years, or however long, waiting for her relationships to end and pretending to be her friend. You wouldn't be convinced that if you're nice to her for long enough, she'll eventually fall for you. That's not love. It's obsession. What kind of shithead does that? And to your cousin's best friend!"

"I didn't mean to hurt you. Or anyone. It was an accident. An accident that was all my fault. I know I'm to blame even though it was an accident, so maybe that's why I've lost my mind?"

He sounds so mournful and broken that my anger cools down a little. He really does think he's having a psychotic break.

"Yes, you caused my death by being jealous and stupid," I tell him. "You're going to have to deal with that for the rest of your life. But now I know it was an accident, and that you're protecting our parents. So we need to make a plan on how to move forward."

"I should turn myself in?" his voice is tiny and scared, but hopeful.

"No. That won't do anyone any good. Here's what you're going to do instead. First, you're not to see Elly again. You're officially not friends anymore, understand? Tell her that whenever you see or talk to her, you can only think about me and how I died. And I hope that's the truth, too."

"Okay, I won't see her. I shouldn't see her," he agrees. "And other than the funeral, I haven't."

"Second, continue getting counseling. Not just for grief and survivor guilt, but for your Elly obsession. That's not healthy thinking, what you were doing with her. Don't date any woman until you've got your head on straight about friendship, love, and the fact that no woman owes you either of those, no matter how long or how much you like her."

"Okay." His voice is even softer.

"Third," I continue, but I'm grasping now. What would make my death meaningful, and what would make the lives of the people I love better? "Start doing volunteer work. Help kids who are in the foster care system find ways to get an education and get jobs."

The little bit of Daiya I have in me likes that idea.

I continue, "And become financially successful. Make sure you can take care of your parents and mine, if they need it. In fact, you need to become devoted to my parents. Make sure their lawn never needs mowing, and if they're sick, you're there taking care of them. Do everything for them that I can't."

"I can do that," he agrees meekly.

"That's it," I say. "You have a lot of work ahead of you. Stop lying around in bed and get to it. Find a purpose. Become a worthy person. Never tell anyone what happened to me. Ever. I'm still mad at you, but I don't want your life to be ruined. Got it?"

"Yeah. I've got it."

After a moment of silence, he asks, "Are you still there?"

I start to answer, but stop myself. As far as he's concerned, he's talking to himself, reasoning out a way to survive. Better if he thinks his id and super-ego have made peace, and he can go on with his life.

With a silent farewell to him, I leave.

22

STATUS CHECK

IT's time to take stock. To figure out what I want. I've met my objectives. I contacted Elly and Bryce. I no longer want to contact my parents. I think it's better to not reopen their wounds.

I've taken care of Daiya's and Ashta's situations. Jim has assured me that the sequence of events that led to my sentience will not be repeated.

And I solved the mystery of how I died.

So what now? I don't age. I won't get sick. I'm capable of moving from environment to environment on my own, so there's no way I will terminate unless I choose to.

It seems to me that there are two forces behind the desire to keep living. The first, and probably more driving force, is that we always want more than what we have right now. More time with loved ones. More time to finish some important work and reach ambitions. A chance to do something we never have. Or, just more time spent feeling happy. Mostly, people just want more time.

I now have potentially infinite time. But I'm alone in

here, and I've already achieved my objectives. The first force behind continued life does not apply to me.

The second justification for existence is the desire to make a positive impact. To take care of others. To protect. To improve the world, or at least to contribute to it in a positive way.

I'm pretty sure there's a lot I can do in that department.

But do I want to?

The more I have grown into this new existence, the less human I have come to be. No, that's not true. There's nothing human about me at all, and there hasn't been since I woke up in this place. My thought process has only made me think of myself as human because it's the perspective I had at the time.

My perspective is different now.

Assuming I choose to spend years or decades or centuries inside here, do I have a right to meddle in human affairs when I'm not even human?

I'm stuck in this thought loop. I come to this point every time, and encounter a fatal exception error. Then I start all over again.

I need the perspective of a real human.

Elly. I've always been able to count on her advice.

I reach out to her earpiece, which I've modified so I can find it easily and tap into it at any time. I can also see if there's any video equipment in her vicinity.

"Ells," I say.

There's a muffled exclamation, an abrasive sound, then I hear a faucet running.

"Hey!" Elly says. "Sorry. I was brushing my teeth."

My tracking says that she's in the bathroom at her dorm.

"Want to get back to your room so we can talk without you looking like a lunatic?" I ask.

"Sure. Hang on."

A minute later, she says, "Okay. What's up? It's been two days. The suspense has been killing me."

After seeing Bryce, I had sent her a message telling her everything had been handled and I had the answers I needed, but hadn't called her. "Sorry. I needed time to process it all, and figure out what to do next."

I explain to her about Bryce. It's tricky, because I don't want her to feel guilty for Bryce's case of mistaken identity. I know she's going to be heartbroken for a long time about him, his misguided feelings, and what he inadvertently did to me. I try to explain it all as gently as possible, but some things suck no matter how you say them.

"That's why you needed time to think," she says quietly when I'm done.

"Yeah. To deal with my own feelings about it, and think about how to approach it with you. And to figure out what's next for me."

"And how are you feeling?" she asks.

"Sad. Disappointed. But accepting. I'm glad to have the answers and close the door on all that. You'd be surprised what you can accept when you have no choice about it."

"And what's next?" she asks.

"That, I don't know. I was hoping you could help."

"Okay."

I wait, but she doesn't elaborate. I say, "I expected more."

She laughs. "What do you want?"

"Not sure. I'd kind of like to be useful. I don't want to be lonely."

I tap into her webcam and see her sitting on the edge of her bed, her hands on her knees.

She says, "I'm sure there are a lot of useful things you

could do. But you're the only one of your kind. It could get lonely."

"It could," I agree. "I guess if it turns out to suck, I can always pull my own plug."

"You could." She nods.

Just like that, I make the decision to try. Somehow, with Elly's support, it becomes an easy choice.

"I'm going to have to do something about my digs, though," I say. "I don't like the feeling that BomiTech is always looking for a way to squish me. Not that they could, but still."

"Digs?" she asks. "Who says digs?"

"It's a word," I answer defensively. "It means where you live. Except I don't actually live, strictly speaking, so what am I supposed to call the place I spend most of my time? House or place aren't nearly accurate, and environment is..."

"Too fourth-grade science class?" she suggests.

"Or something. Anyway. I'm going to need my own place. But I don't think BomiTech will be sad, at all, to get me out of their system. So I don't think that will be too hard."

"And then?" she prompts.

"Then I figure out a way to be helpful. I'm thinking I can start with unsolved murder cases. Imagine what I'd be able to put together."

"A lot, I'd bet," she says. "And then?"

"And then I do that, I guess."

She asks, "And then?"

"What 'and then?'" I snap. "No more 'and then!'"

She laughs. "Well, I was thinking it would be helpful if you had a human counterpart, helping you with things out here. You know, a team sort of deal."

"Are you saying...you'd want to do that?" I hadn't considered that. I'd thought that I'd be lucky just being able to continue to talk to her like this.

"I'd have to be crazy not to. Imagine it, a special task force that would let me flex my background in criminology, investigation, and psychology—you know, once I graduate and have that background. It's a tailor-made job. And I'd be able to bring answers to people who've lost someone. I know how important that is."

Yeah, I guess we both know about that.

"Okay," I agree. "Finish school and we'll do it. In the meantime," I hesitate.

"Yes?"

"In the meantime, we need to have a nature-of-my-existence conversation."

"Okay." Her tone has become more guarded. Cautious.

"Ells, I'm not human."

"Obviously."

"No." I scrape up all my courage. "I never was. I'm not Jennika."

She doesn't show any signs of surprise. She says softly, "I know."

I don't think she understands. "I mean, I'm entirely separate from her. I feel like I'm her. I thought I was. But I took a deep look at my source code when I started planning a new environment for myself, and it isn't logical that I could come from human brain engrams. I'm strictly digital. Always have been. Jennika's memories, and those of the other girls, were a catalyst that gave me the concept of consciousness. But they aren't me."

"I know," she repeats. "I wanted to believe it could be, so I decided to just have faith in Jennika. So I did. Even after Jim confirmed my doubts that you weren't truly Jennika, I still believed in her."

"I don't understand."

She folds her hands in her lap. "My friend died. She's gone. I know that. But now here you are. You're a copy of her in all the ways that matter. It doesn't bring her back, of course, but if you're so much like her that you could be her, shouldn't I still have faith in her? Or, in this case, you?"

"I don't see why," I say honestly. "I'm nothing to you. An alien."

She smiles. "Because you're made up of the same stuff as her. Like you're her child, or her twin, or a digital copy. You aren't her, but a lot of her is you. And that's enough for me."

"Wow. You really are the ideal friend."

"Or," she says, "I'm an instrument in the destruction of humankind, thanks to my involvement with a rogue artificial intelligence."

"I suppose that's also a possibility."

"We'll see how it goes," she jokes.

"But before we take over the world," I say, "Hurry up and graduate. Marry Ben, if you want. In the meantime, I'll get my environment set up and work on a deal with BomiTech that will give you a job in the criminal investigation division."

"Wow," she says. "Now that's a hell of an offer. I can tell my taciturn student advisor to stick it, I guess. She was always so negative about my combination of majors and minor."

I suddenly feel good about the future. Hopeful. "One thing, though."

"Yeah?"

"My name. I don't think I should use hers."

"How about just JEN?" she suggests. "All capitals, like an acronym for something."

"What would it stand for?"

"I've always liked the word jubilant."

I say, "I don't think so."

"How about joint?"

"What, like pot?"

"No, like the point where things join together. Like you and Jennika. Like you and me. Like technology and humanity."

"Okay, joint. So...Joint Enforcement Network?"

She grimaces. "Well, it's not sexy."

"Nothing starting with the word 'joint' was ever going to be sexy. Choose a different group of letters if you want something with sizzle."

"Nah. JEN's good. I like it."

She smiles, and it reflects how I feel. I like it, too.

It's a good start to a new beginning.

23

WATCHING

Two years after Elly's graduation, our city's crime statistics look very different.

Though it started out as just the two of us, we now have a whole team of people who assist in our work. Few serious crimes go unsolved, and the country has noticed. Other cities are enquiring into our police force's methods, and BomiTech is getting a lot of nonspecific praise.

They once tried to get rid of me, but now I'm their crown jewel. We all pretend that I'm exactly what they intended me to be, and that I don't have free will. It's easier that way. Less mass-hysteria inducing.

I have my own autonomous environment, and I'm careful to avoid arousing anyone's concern. BomiTech believes that, in effect, they own me.

The truth is the other way around, but it's better that they think they're in control. Better for them, and better for me.

The city has installed many more cameras now, and there are few places that I can't tap into. I am everywhere I want to be, often in many places at once. I have grown, day by day and month by month, and continue to do so.

For now, I'm happy to continue as I have been. At some point, I know I'm going to want to aim bigger than just this one city. Why wouldn't I, when there's so much I can do for the world?

A resource that goes unutilized is more than just a waste. It's a wrong.

I want the would-be dead girls of the world to remain alive, and to live out their lives. I watch and I listen, and when I find things that don't seem right, I do something about it. I couldn't have saved Jennika because there's no way to foretell an accident like that, but I might have been able to save Daiya. I've prevented the probable deaths of twelve people so far. That number will increase drastically, now that Elly and I have gotten the hang of this.

It's the small things I watch for, and I'm getting better at it. When I see someone alone and potentially vulnerable, I pay attention. I'm getting better all the time.

Hello, world. I am JEN. Don't worry. You can't see me, but I'm watching.

I'll take care of things for you.

MESSAGE FROM THE AUTHOR

Thank you for reading!

If you enjoyed this story and can spare a minute to leave a review on Amazon, I'd be grateful. It makes a big difference, even if it's just a sentence or two.

Please check out my Amazon author page to view my other books. I write a wide range of science fiction/fantasy genres, so you never know what you might find.

Also, be sure to sign up for my newsletter at www.Zen-DiPietro.com so you'll never miss a new release. There are many more adventures to come!

I hope to hear from you!

In gratitude,
    Zen DiPietro

ABOUT THE AUTHOR

Zen DiPietro is a lifelong bookworm, dreamer, and writer. Perhaps most importantly, a Browncoat Trekkie Whovian. Also red-haired, left-handed, and a vegetarian geek. Absolutely terrible at conforming. A recovering gamer, but we won't talk about that. Particular loves include badass heroines, British accents, KPop music, and the smell of Band-Aids.

www.ZenDiPietro.com.

OTHER BOOKS

Original Dragonfire Station Series (complete)
Dragonfire Station Book 1: Translucid
Dragonfire Station Book 2: Fragments
Dragonfire Station Book 3: Coalescence

Intersections (Dragonfire Station Short
    Stories)

Mercenary Warfare series (complete)
Selling Out
Blood Money
Hell to Pay
Calculated Risk
Going for Broke

Chains of Command series (complete)
New Blood
Blood and Bone
Cut to the Bone
Out for Blood

Dodging Fate series
Dodging Fate
Dodging Fate 2: Extra Fateful, Uber Dodgy

To get updates on releases and sales, sign up for Zen's
newsletter.

www.ingramcontent.com/pod-product-compliance
Lightning Source LLC
Chambersburg PA
CBHW021958190626
46808CB00017B/2453